Dark Roots

*For Louise Thurtell and Peter Bishop,
both of whom refuse to believe that
the short story is an endangered species*

DARK ROOTS

CATE KENNEDY

BLACK CAT
New York
a paperback original imprint of Grove/Atlantic Inc.

First Published in Australia in 2006 by Scribe Publications Pty Ltd

Published simultaneously in Canada
Printed in the United States of America

ISBN-10: 0-8021-7045-5
ISBN-13: 978-0-8021-7045-3

Black Cat
a paperback original imprint of Grove/Atlantic, Inc.
841 Broadway
New York, NY 10003
Distributed by Publishers Group West
www.groveatlantic.com
08 09 10 11 12   10 9 8 7 6 5 4 3 2 1

Contents

'There is some secret grief here I need to declare,
and my fingers itch for a pencil.'
—Barbara Kingsolver

What Thou and I Did, Till We Loved

Every day I go to get off at the wrong floor. I keep forgetting. She's in rehab now. They've given her six weeks in here, to assess progress, testing all the reflexes and how hard her hands can squeeze. After that, well, we'll have to see, they say. They mean moving her to a permanent residential facility. Those are the actual words they use; they are good at jargon, of course; that is their job.

'I think your reaction is a little emotive and inappropriate,' they say; or, 'We're trying to find the most constructive way forward for patient recovery.'

I sit next to Beth's bed and think up jargon for her, whispering.

'Would you care to listen to your mobile melody-generating headset device?' I say, holding her Walkman near her ear, watching her eyes.

'Can you indicate if you would like a drink from your cold-beverage receptacle?' I persist, although of course she cannot sip and swallow, liquids trickle into her body via a tube. Watching her mouth for some flicker of a smile, of recognition. Some days her eyes are open, sometimes not. It is inappropriate, they tell me, to use the term 'awake' on the occasions she opens her eyes. Some other brain activity is occurring. There is no fevered one-blink-for-yes-two-blinks-for-no or finger-jabbing at letters on a newspaper page. There is nothing but this.

I talk, talk, talk. On bad days I believe them, because if she were sentient those eyes would be flashing out messages like a lighthouse: *SOS. Shipwreck.* There would not be this slow breathing, but tears of frustration, the hand she can move would flail the air, grab for something. Instead she is like a body relieved of its burden of energy, suspended. All seven patients in this room lie like islands, and whatever is shifting is deep under the surface. I check her charts, see what they've been subjecting her to in rehab—needles in the feet and hands, maybe, flashlight in the eyes. I don't know. 'Nil by mouth' is what it says, which is the truth. Nothing going in. Nothing coming out.

That first day in intensive care when I'd arrived, one of the staff had asked if I was next-of-kin and I'd taken a shuddering breath and craned over her shoulder where I could see Beth's bag and shoes next to the bed and her head inconceivably, impossibly, angled into that brace. They had her shopping bag there, everything in it intact. And jammed in the top, a bunch of flowers she'd been holding when the taxi hit her. They'd been six hours out of water and looking at them I glimpsed things as they would be from now on. The diodes pinching, monitoring, and the new glittery, chromium, machine-fed rules of helplessness. And my mouth waited to set this horror in motion, and I opened it and said: *sister, yes, her sister.* I would have said anything.

I get here around 8.30 a.m. Link fingers in Beth's, tell her about my trip down, the news I'd heard on the radio, anything. Such luxuriant amounts of time in this room; it stretches and balloons like molten glass.

Each day, stepping blindly out of chaos. I have left my catering business in an uproar, gathered up the mail and dumped it in the top drawer, ignored the calls waiting on the answering machine.

Usually at this time of the morning I am selecting asparagus or stuffing capsicums, faxing the client to check how many vegetarians I should expect. We stack the random CD player and the industrial kitchen starts pumping. Nowadays it pumps in an entirely different way, like an artery losing blood, with my friend David the chef trying to instruct the two trainees from the employment service to hold things together, the three of them hapless as failing tourniquets. My business has fading vital signs; it is anaemic with lost clientele and drastically slipped standards. I, the chief surgeon, am standing gravely by, stripping off my rubber gloves.

When I press the stored number in the mobile phone the auto-dial sounds like the manic music before a cartoon. David and the trainees never answer. My own voice on the voicemail greets me, cheery as a head waiter covering up the bedlam behind the swinging doors. I try again, holding the handset against my sweater so I don't have to hear that inane little loony tunes series of chirps. On with the show, this is it.

It was how I met Beth, actually, through catering. A university function, in the days when you couldn't move in the food business without falling over a tray of sushi. Moroccan lamb was what I served that day, rice with preserved lemons, semolina cake. Big, satisfying carbohydrates. I'd left the faculty conference and wandered past a lecture theatre. She was up on the podium, reading poetry. To a roomful of restless undergraduates, who were doodling on their handouts and eyeing the clock. I stood there leaning against the door, thinking that the Dean could serve his own cake.

'Look over here,' says the physio, and she snaps her fingers, watching Beth's eyes, which are gazing up at the ceiling. A ponderous, slow-motion blink. I will the eyes to turn to meet the physio's snapping, to have them snap back angrily, absolutely alert. I imagine Beth saying, *Yes, what?* in that impatient way she has when she is focused on something else, imagine the physio staggering backwards in shock.

Another blink, a kind of sigh. I bend my head near. Sometimes Beth's mouth forms a meandering string of vowels, slippery as water in a creek, the consonants that would make them words buried in that sleeping tongue.

The first time it had happened was after a big mob of friends came in, back in the other room, and we'd all stood joking around her bed, behaving as if we were all standing round at a party but that Beth was engaged in some obscure performance piece of her own secret devising. We needed to out-act her.

We brushed her hair and burned aromatherapy oils and turned her hands over in our own, and when visiting hours were finished and they had left, Beth spoke, very softly, and from far away, the clotted remnants of two words: *no more*.

Now the physio goes back to folding her arms as I bend to Beth's cheek and hear the breathy vowel, deadened, exhaled. Is it *no*? Or is it *go*?

'She's not talking,' says the physio. 'Please don't get your hopes up.'

Tell that bitch to go, maybe. That's what I hope.

'They're not romantic poets,' Beth said to me as we sat at my place on that first night and demolished the remains of the cake. 'They're the metaphysical poets. It was the golden age of the English Renaissance.' She laced those long fingers together, those hands that looked like they could pluck birds out of the air. 'Donne's the one. Body and spirit.'

She had cake crumbs on her lower lip, and as she spoke it struck me that I'd been married to my ex for seven years and would never have waited like this, perfectly content, to see whether he would lick them off.

'Headfirst into the riddle of intellect and love,' she was saying, and then she paused, and grinned at me. 'Great cake,' she added.

I reached over and brushed off the crumbs. I'd known her

seven hours. And the ghostly, amazed remnant apparition of me who had been standing in the corner of the kitchen monitoring all this, aghast, turned around and walked out and I never heard from her again.

It was as easy as that.

I'm looking at those lips now, a thin line like a curve you would cut into pastry.

I wonder, by my troth, she had recited in that lecture, *what thou and I Did, till we loved? Were we not wean'd till then? But suck'd on country pleasures, childishly? Or snorted we in the Seven Sleepers' den?*

I watch her face, talking. Her voluptuous thighs have become thin under the sheet, her hipbones protrude. Her food bag looks filled with puree of vegetables, something you sieve into a baby's mouth out of a can. The tube they have inserted into her to receive this nourishment disappears under the sheet. 'Careful, careful of all those tubes,' the nurses are forever warning me, as if I'm going to lunge on her, crawl into bed beside her. Fit my body alongside hers there in the white envelope bed and by osmosis absorb her through my skin — Beth, my food and drink. For now I hold only her hand, feeling faint spasms ripple through it like a fish nibbling on a line, those fingers always seeming on the verge of gesture.

I could pick her up now and carry her, away from the baby food and the other six patients, slumbering on, out of this hermetic den. The door would resist, then the airlock would surrender, letting oxygen in.

I sit and feel the spell overtake me, my head jerking backwards, awake and stricken.

'You should go home,' says a nurse, carrying bedding in. 'You need ...'

She is going to say some sleep, but under the circumstances, amends it to rest.

At home I will listen at last to the string of messages David will have left on the machine.

'Hate to do this to you,' he'll start, 'but one of us has to make petit fours, believe it or not, for the Professional Women's Network tomorrow. Rebecca, the last time I saw a petit four I was the only boy in Home Economics class. I'm ... well, ring me. Will you?'

I would have said once that I am a person who revels in the time-consuming. I used to do things like stuff mushrooms, make all the stocks from scratch, rub sugar cubes into orange peel while watching TV because I don't think you can get that zest flavour any other way.

The day Beth had the accident, I was doing something which just had to have black sesame seeds, and I called out to her, busy planing down a new back step, and asked her if she'd run down to Nicholson Street and get me some. I had to lift the headphones away from her ears to ask again, and I remember the glossy slip of her hair between my fingers, her nod, her tucking money into her jeans and going out on that foolish chore. Black sesame seeds, as if the world would stop if I didn't have them. And the sun in the kitchen, listening to PBS, and the time lengthening and lengthening.

Sharpening into fear. And the phone ringing.

The sequence of events locking into place around that phone call, what came before and what came after, has dislocated something in me.

Because now I am another person. I am someone who drags her feet like she was underwater down to the 24-hour Safeway, for blocks of plain, commercial yellow cake and home-brand cocoa powder, and I stand at the same kitchen table at midnight constructing counterfeit petit fours that fool nobody, that taste like nothing, that sit there like stage props.

I watch my hands make them with a distant fascination that something like this ever engaged me. I marvel that the human brain can be bothered to store the knowledge of how to do it, the brain that can know how to select a bolt to secure a step, listen to music, remember poetry and, with enough impact and under enough duress, be switched off as suddenly as a current.

I am a person, now, who sits and holds a wrist and tries to inhale a scent that's been leached out from skin that tastes of antibiotic and somehow, impossibly, of that yellow, cottony cake.

Do I want to climb into that bed and take my turn forgetting, to look inwards into the hazy darkness of that cave? I do. Yes, I do.

It pumps out of me, my will. I lift Beth a little in her bed and feel her flesh move across her glutinous bones like fabric, her muscles dissolved away. I know she is using up stored energy now, that as she respires she is converting all those past meals eaten. I have plenty of time to consider this, breathing the sweet cellared-apple smell of her breath. This whole room reeks of hibernation. My exhaustion pours into the void, chatters to itself, bends towards that thick pure silence of disengagement. It is almost spring now, and I have brought some jonquils into this room. Their cut stems ooze viscous fluid like plasma, their scent wafts in tiny measured exhalations, like the invisible ticking of a clock.

At home I cook her favourite soup and relive the last time I made it. She had sat at the kitchen table, reading bits out of the paper. I see her hand reach over and take a pear, and that wicked smile.

'There's something so sensuous,' she had sighed, draping herself mockingly over the table, 'about a woman eating a pear.' Those teeth, sliding into brown skin.

Now I put the soup into the blender, garnish and all, and pour it into a plastic jug—a smooth, pale puree that disguises every ingredient. This is the thing about cooking: its labour is invisible. It's a gift you absorb without noticing, storing it away for when the winter finally hits.

I have what I want to say worked out, but when the charge sister finally pushes open the door I can only turn the jug on the laminex table and stutter something.

'I'm afraid it's not possible,' she says. She's not unkind. On this floor there are thirty-three people like Beth, and she must weigh and measure her compassion out, like medication.

'It's only soup,' I say. 'Almost exactly like what you already give her. Just vegetables. I'm a cook.'

'What we give the patient,' she says, 'is perfectly nutritionally balanced.'

Beth's hand lies in mine like an empty glove just discarded by someone warm.

'Sister,' I begin, and she shakes her head regretfully. I am not being constructive. I am being unhelpful. The young nurse accompanying her rubs slowly at the sink with a spotless towel, and, when the charge sister leaves, comes over and sits on the bed.

'Sorry,' she says. 'It smells great, whatever it is.'

Beth's lips are parted like someone in an opium dream. Under her bluish lids I see eye movement. *If ever any beauty I did see*, she had said that day, *Which I desired, and got, 'twas but a dream of thee.* I had given her an old edition of a collection of John Donne's, last year, our paper anniversary. I was expecting a cookbook from her, a lush edition I had seen and told her about, but her gift to me was a page in an envelope, and I had that page now in my bag, folded among the other documents and bills and residential-care stipulations, because what she had given me was a new will naming me, among other things, as her medical power of attorney. Beth, Beth. Headfirst into the riddle.

'How old are you?' I say to the nurse.

'Nineteen.'

'What time do you finish this shift?'

'Five in the morning,' she answers, and I'm opening my mouth to tell her that she'd better have the soup, when a ribbon of sound emerges from Beth's lips, her breathing jerks and a little grunt of effort starts it up again.

I lean down. 'Tell me again,' I whisper. 'I missed it.'

The noise drifts again from her throat: four vowels lifted from the air, the mouth wadded with loss. The young nurse's face lights up.

'Did you hear that?' she says.

'Yeah.'

'Can you work out what she said?'

I hesitate. I am so tired, Beth. I want my own oblivion from this savage procession of images; of a bag of shopping untouched while you lie ruined, of some ambulance officer prising your fingers one by one from the bunch of lilies you'd bought (for me, for me), of that step I have left just as it was, so that each time I go outside I stumble, my ankle jarring, tripping over the black hole of something inexplicably seized.

'What do you think she said?' I answer at last.

The nurse blinks. 'She said, "I love you." Didn't she?'

'Yes,' I say. 'Take that soup with you. Please. Help yourself.'

So I am left alone with you again, out of visiting hours, three days until our deadline, as you slumber in this cave, this room that is an everywhere. What did we do, till we loved, Beth, and what will we do now? Maybe when I was nineteen I would have believed that if the power of speech could be mustered with such effort, it could be squandered on declarations of love, but I know you, and so I know better now.

Take out this tube is what you said to me. *Take out this tube.*

How is it that I can want to sleep, as I walk through my kitchen at 2.00 a.m? Here is the wreckage of preparation, of dishes piled and unwashed, of a red light flashing on an answering machine like an abandoned satellite signalling for re-entry somewhere, anywhere. Here are debts in unopened envelopes, the slow drifting swansong of resignation. And here is a plane and a set of drill bits, a piece of timber leaning against the back door, a small pile of wood shavings I scoop into my hand before stepping carefully over that dark gap and sitting down.

I raise them to my face and inhale as I sit there, smelling forest which is gone now, a breathing tree turned mute and felled and unrecognisable, nothing but lumber.

A Pitch Too High for the Human Ear

If I signed off at 4.50 I could take the 5.00 p.m. bus and be home in time to help Matthew with his maths and peel the potatoes while Vicki moved around the kitchen doing everything else. We'd turn the TV round on its console, like one of those things in a Chinese restaurant, and watch the six o'clock news together, hardly ever commenting on it. Baths and a story. Another beer at 9.00 and I'd already be thinking of tomorrow. It was that kind of tiredness you get from doing nothing all day, the exhaustion of sitting. When I married I was a fairly handy forward with the Cougars—B Grade, scored 174 baskets one season. Now I drove my kids to sports, stood on windy sidelines hearing parents scream at their eight-year-olds to get in and kill him. Sometimes I'd still be awake at 3.00 a.m. or so, usually Sunday nights, lying there unstretched, cramped up and watching the smooth outline of my wife dreaming something else nearby.

This is how you slide from a bed: move your foot out and over the edge, find the floor, slide sideways supporting yourself on the bedside table, your fingers touching the fake antique lamp your parents gave you a pair of for a wedding present. Haul out from under the doona. Carry your runners and put them on outside the back door, with your dog already leaping at the thought of what's ahead, way down at the gate. You can just see, in the moonlight, that strange red-gold glint, like road reflectors, from the dog's eyes. Ecstatic to be out, to be marauding, to be running.

When I was in training, before I was married, I used to run four or five kilometres a night sometimes, around the deserted cul-de-sacs in the suburbs when they were so new there were no streetlights. I'd learned to drive in the same streets, reverse parking down battleaxe driveways of barely finished houses, doing hill starts up in the high parts of the new residential zone. Look out beyond the landscaping of roads then, and there were paddocks full of agisted horses. Now the shrubs were higher than your head, there were cars in every drive, ten buses a day, a new health centre. Five kilometres then, with a sense I could have kept going out past the cleared blocks and sewer trenches and run straight into the hills. Now I was flagging after three, barely making it to the service station on the corner of the expressway, looking at the yellow neon of the 24-hour drive-through McDonalds where the horses used to be. Fourteen years—what's that? Two kids, a wedding photo where you can't believe the suit you wore, and the golden arches.

We'd got Kelly when he was two years old from a workmate who said he needed a lot of exercise, whose relief I could feel as he brushed dog hair off his car's upholstery and declined a beer.

He was a sucker for the dead-of-night runs, Kelly. Heeler-cross, and I never saw him tire. On Sunday nights when *Disneyland* was on, Kelly would be pressing himself to the back door, staring inside with such longing that Louise and Matthew would beg Vicki until she'd relent, and they'd slide open the glass door and Kelly would be allowed to come in, so abject and grateful he'd be practically crawling, licking our hands, cramming himself between the kids, and Vicki saying, *Look just leave him alone and he'll calm down, kids, just relax and stop mucking round with him*, but finally something would be overturned and Kelly would be outside again, and it would be, *Okay now, time for bed, school tomorrow*, the dog staring in through the glass with desperate remorse. You could hear him, sometimes, this barely audible high whine, still as a statue, only a muscle in his throat giving him away.

Half past three in the morning, though, and Kelly was beautiful to watch, down across the footy oval and up the hill, turning around to recover the ground back to me, a long shape in the moonlight. He'd streak past me, and out of the darkness I'd feel him nudge my hand in passing as he came forward again; he could have gone all night, barrelling into the sleeping suburbs. I'd pound up those streets with my chest hurting, my feet feeling like sinkers, knowing I'd never score 174 again. Catching my breath at the servo,

Kelly would go round behind the 7–11 and root through the weekend garbage, and nobody was there to give a shit.

Here's how you get into a bed without waking the other person: flush the toilet and come back in as if you're practically sleepwalking, fold back the sheet so that it doesn't disturb them, slowly straighten out your legs under it, and watch the red digital numbers change from 5.15 to 5.16, to 5.17. They're so silent they're eerie, digital clocks—it's as if time is not passing after all, just kind of rolling.

Why don't we talk more, after the kids are in bed? is what Vicki used to say. Then it became *why don't you talk more*, then *oh, Andrew, he never talks. Don't bother*, Vicki would say at the barbecues we went to, to other women drinking wine on the folding chairs. *I married a non-talker.*

When she stopped talking, though, when she got so jack of it she closed up and just worked silently in the kitchen like a black cloud, I could hardly stand it. I would rather have her filling in the blank spots, even complaining, even shouting, than silent. Spreading butter on bread, on the eighteen rows of sandwiches she was going to put in the freezer so that you'd know for a week it was going to be devon and tomato sauce, then cheese and ham, things that froze well, so careful with placing the squares against the crust of the bread, saying, *Andrew this is just crazy, I'm going to have to do a night course or something to get out of the house.* Tucking the corners back on the sandwich bags, wiping the back of her hand against her eyes like she thought the kids wouldn't notice. Watching her, a hundred things came into my mind to say that I discarded, everything staying unsaid—like when Matt was born and we just sat there looking at each other. The difference was then it didn't seem to matter, me being something that she used to call inarticulate and she now called withholding.

Ham and cheese, ham and cheese, ham and cheese, seed mustard on Dad's, chutney on the kids'. I couldn't take my eyes from her hands, remembered them squeezing mine on our wedding day as I'd stood up to make my speech, the culmination of four days of nervous diarrhoea. *I married a non-talker*, Vicki saying with a tight smile at parties, or silently flicking through the channels with the remote as I wracked my brain for something to say that would make her talk again. *How can you just* stand *there?* Vicki said now, sawing the sandwiches with the knife. *I don't know*, I answered, which was the honest truth.

Twelve years of night running, working the bolt open silently on the back gate, watching Kelly let rip.

When we started the oval had opened out to empty land, now there was a maze of clothes lines, fences, paved patios. When the dog disappeared up the incline on the other side, he'd pause and turn, waiting for me. I could whistle so softly it was barely audible and he'd instantly race back like a rocket. Incredible hearing, turning towards the sound like a dish picking up radar. Outside the back door, ears straining through the glass, he'd hear his name and start shaking with excitement, picking up his front feet like they were hot, trying to sit up straight like a kid waiting to be let out of school. *Oh please, Mum*, Louise would plead. *Please let him.* My soft-hearted Lou.

I got promoted. Matthew got taller and sat hunched over his Nintendo GameBoy instead of practising soccer. Vicki did two nights a week at TAFE: Write Your Life Story, Crystal Healing, Thai Cooking, Start Your Own Small Business, The Tarot and You, Stretch Sewing.

One year I was opening and unfolding the Christmas tree and remembered that I'd meant to fix the two broken branches with fishing line a few months before. No — it had been a year ago. It couldn't be a year since Christmas but it was; the same jammed aisles of $2 crap, worrying what Vicki would like, thirty-six shopping hours to go, going crazy with the muzak. If you'd have asked me what I'd wanted, I couldn't have said.

It had been different — I was sure it had been — when the kids believed in Santa. Vicki and I had drunk port together and eaten the shortbread, scattered the grass clippings Louise had arranged in little piles for the reindeer, listened to the carols on TV, gone into the bedrooms and looked at our kids sleeping, feeling sentimental and exhausted from setting up train sets and fairy outfits in the lounge room. Kids believe in Santa; adults believe in childhood.

Then it was January the second of a New Year we didn't stay up for, and I was back to work on the twelfth, and in that time would be a week at the coast, and in the middle of the night I'm watching the digital numbers shift like blinking and I get up and get my runners. Kelly's curled up on the back mat, and wakes up from a deep sleep when I touch him and looks surprised. He stands and stretches, runs a bit stiffly down to the gate to wait, and it seems like the same kind of strange joke that only such a short time ago you couldn't keep him down; he leapt from that guy's car into our front yard with so much energy. Now he takes off down the street and I stop at the end to rest a stitch that feels like a deep knot in my gut pulling upwards, and I jog to the oval and see Kelly trotting slowly to the incline on the far side. I am forty-two years old and the kind of guy who once scored 174 baskets in a season but now gives his wife a StaySharp knife for Christmas, who can barely jog two kilometres, who can never think of what to say, and none of it really hits me until I whistle to watch Kelly bolting back down across the grass and he doesn't come. He is turned towards me and seems to be waiting, he seems to pick me out in the darkness and know what has always happened before, but he shakes his head, gives a nervous yawn and I realise he can't hear me; he's deaf.

It seems a little extreme, the vet said to me. *Lots of dogs with impaired hearing continue to enjoy a good quality of life.* Kelly lying there, looking at nothing. Not impaired, silent. I watched the vet click his fingers behind the dog, clap, whistle. *Sometimes,* he said, *this kind of thing's hereditary.* He got out a kind of tuning fork and struck it against his desk and tried again. *This is at a pitch too high for the human ear,* he said, telling me about frequency range and how maybe it was only partial, how I'd have to watch out now for traffic and keep him on a leash, how often heelers live to a ripe old age, and Kelly, deaf, stiff and fifteen years old — it suddenly struck me like a train — didn't stir once. *But you're going to have to start thinking soon ...* said the vet, and I interrupted him.

Do it now, I said.

Driving home, it felt like something was strangling me, a muscle tight as a wire in my throat, giving me away, a sound escaping like one long word. The only word.

God, how could you? How could you? Vicki kept saying, rocking Louise on the couch. I couldn't open my mouth, for fear of what might come out. The compression of unsaid things filling my chest, lungs hurting for air. *Don't you have any feelings at all*, she said. It was Matthew that had the nightmares after that, in the week we didn't go to the coast. We both jumped to get up to him, both grimly solicitous, comforting, heating milk, suddenly keen to outdo each other as the better parent, as if we both knew what was ahead. Passing each other in the hall we might as well have been two strangers on the bus, standing to let the other pass with a brittle courtesy that made me know it was finally over.

He had the kids' dog put down, Vicki would say at barbecues now, *without even telling them. The family dog. Andrew just had so many unresolved issues.*

This would be later, after Vicki had counselling.

Wednesday afternoons I work through till 6.00 and drive out to the stadium for the match. The Westside Wranglers, middle of the ladder, and none of us tries too hard. Every guy in the team is my age, sick of jogging, nursing some minor nagging injury that requires liniment and strapping, and only three of us are still married. Sunday afternoons we train half-heartedly with lots of familiar banter and then on the weekends I don't have custody of the kids I drink stubbies with them in the social club while we watch the A-grade women's teams on the courts below us. The sounds seem to distort, hitting the high hangar ceiling — the whistles and shouts and squeaks of people's shoes as they pound up and down — sound bending like it's coming through water.

I watch people sometimes, wonder how they can walk around with the weight of what they know. Wonder if they feel like me, stumbling with lead shoes on the bottom of the ocean, swimming in a sea of the unsayable. It's a mistake we make, thinking it's words that tell us everything. It's sound that breaks glasses, cracks windows, sends cats up trees. Bats hear more than humans, understand more noise, let alone dogs. Maybe we're just not getting it, standing here listening for sensible speech, dying of loneliness and waiting for whatever it is. How do we know we're not calling and calling all the time, our throats so tight with it, it's too high to hear? At night I hear dogs barking, and think how much of their howling is outside my conscious range, so that I feel it like a vibration but mistake it for silence? Sitting in the club, turning my fourth and last stubbie on the laminex, I want to phone my ex-wife. I want to say her name and then hold the receiver into air, let her listen to the roar of everything we can't bear to hear.

Can you hear it Vicki? I want to say. It's not words, it's nothing so coherent as words. It's all of us, hoarse with calling, straining in the darkness to hear something we recognise as our names.

Habit

I've never been much good at reading the fine print on cards, least of all after a 28-hour flight. But now that I was actually carrying three kilos of cocaine, I read the customs declaration form with, you might say, a whole new vested interest. Any illegal or contraband goods? Well, you'd have to be pretty jetlagged to fall into that trap, wouldn't you? Tick no. Any weaponry? Any exotic flora or fauna? They must think we're idiots, says the person next to me, an insufferable bore in black leather pants which have squeaked ever since we left Singapore.

Well, no, they don't think we're idiots. It's the only way of nailing us if we're carrying anything, otherwise we can plead ignorance of the law. I don't tell him this, of course. It would be an open provocation to continue talking to me, and the last thing I want is another instalment of his failed marriage. I seem to be inviting confession and disclosure—people have been doing it to me since boarding the first plane in Bogotá. My silence only seems to encourage them.

I am steeling myself also for the three questions, the three biggies they hit you with as your suitcase hits the examination table. Is this your luggage? Did you pack it yourself? Are you aware of its contents? Then they pull open the zip and all bets are off—you're cactus. Foolish carriers, in these intolerably stressful circumstances, take a couple of tranks to settle their nerves for this ordeal. Personally I can't think of anything that would give me away more than pinhole pupils and a Mogadon stupor.

I suppose I should say a few words about the cocaine. An illegal drug, certainly, but a word in my defence, your Honour. I have, I suppose, a habit. If you can call three snorts a habit, because they instilled in me a craving for the drug that surpassed mere physical hankering. Three years ago I tried some street coke and the hit was just enough, through the glucodin and speed percentage that seared into my nasal cavities, to make me make a vow to myself. I decided that if I ever had the chance, I would try the real thing: the purest, whitest Colombian cocaine available to the casual buyer.

As I said, that was a few years ago now, at a party where most people were on the nod around the room with alcohol and dope. With narcotic drugs, in fact. Ridiculously, cocaine is also classified as a narcotic drug, and that evening illustrated for me that misnomer, the vast gulf between its effects and those of alcohol. Me and a few friends mashed the grass down in the backyard with our dancing. I went straight from the party to work and put in a good day. When I got home and pondered on my energy, rapier-like memory retention and sparkling intellect, I made the decision that if one day I had nothing to lose, I'd make the trip myself and take the risk, and buy enough coke to last me the distance.

And it's not long to go now, that distance. I have a trusted doctor, Dr Mick I-won't-tell-you-his-last-name, who'll keep me out of jail, if it comes to that, on humanitarian grounds: he'll show the court the X-rays, the images of the shadow and its advance, and the judge's heart will be wrung with sympathy. At least that's what I'm banking on. A year, eighteen months, whatever it is, I want to spend it full of energy and memory and sparkle, not dry-retching into a bucket after pointless chemotherapy.

So here I am on the plane, inviting intimate disclosures from the squeaker, my pen toying over the box that will seal my fate. Have you anything to declare? Well, yes, as a matter of fact I have. I declare that if I get out of this airport intact, undiscovered, I will put one bag of cocaine aside and savour the rest slowly, sit up at night feeling awake and powerful and not sick; and write letters to everyone I need to, to be opened at the party at which my will will be read out. My will, for what it's worth. My spotless record as a youth worker has left me with no assets besides a VCR so ancient that no one can repair it and that no one in their right mind would steal, a flat full of furniture that may as well go straight back down to the St Vinnies and a collection of books that friends will find are mostly theirs anyway. Not even a car. I sold the car, to pay for the airline ticket to South America.

So sue me. And for the cocaine, I cashed in my super. Hell, you may as well spend it while you've got it—you can't take it with you. No indeed.

I've read up a lot about cocaine. A wonder drug, mistreated cruelly. More sinned against than sinning. More maligned upon than malignant. A perfect anaesthetic, and, many exponents say, completely non-habit-forming. I will give that theory a run for its money, and get back to you. If there's an addiction to be had, I volunteer to be the one to take it on. I go now bravely where no one has gone before, fully cognisant.

In fact in all respects without parallel, it seems to me, except as a painkiller. No, heroin must take that crown. Hence the third bag. The Exchange Bag.

Many years ago there was a preparation available in hospices for terminally ill patients called Brompton's Mixture, which alleviated both the pain and the terror of dying, and it was composed—you can look this up if you like—of cocaine and heroin. Brompton's Cocktail. Brompton's Elixir. The gods must quaff this in heaven. I'm not ashamed to say that this information, about the painkilling, played a big part in my decision. I've taken enough paracetamol to make my kidneys unfit for organ donation, even if anyone was stupid enough to want to take them.

'I'm not looking forward to the pain side of things,' I told Dr Mick.

'There's always morphine,' he said, and I imagined myself, in a bed crisp as blank paper, tubes up my nose and in my arms, souped to the eyeballs on morphine and trying to tell my friends what I thought of them. Not a good look. Not at all. I want to be jolly and on my feet and full of the kind of wit that people will repeat at my wake. I'm only thirty-two, God help me. I want to mash the grass down with my dancing, and one day fall as gracefully as a leaf. Once you decide to take a risk with a clear head and full knowledge of all possible consequences, you're filled with calm.

'I don't want any of these drugs,' I had told Dr Mick with a firm resolve, gesturing to his happy little chart of radiotherapy and chemotherapy treatments. 'You've said yourself that it's too far gone.'

'Well, I shouldn't have said that,' he replied, in a miracles-can-happen voice.

'I'll choose my own drugs,' I'd said, and at that point the Colombian option had occurred to me.

'Well, you let me know if there's anything I can do for you,' he'd replied sombrely. And I'd looked over at him, suddenly remembering doctors were allowed to sign passport applications.

The thing is, I still feel reasonably okay. On a sunny day when you're about to start a descent through angel clouds to land back in your hometown, it's just too hard to comprehend. I have an image of this thing on my X-rays, and it's low and it's dark. And so I will combat it, with high and white. Narcotrafico. My magic crystals. The no-smoking lights go on and I tune back into the guy next to me, who's setting off a volley of new squeaks as he settles into his seatbelt.

'I don't suppose you've ever smoked,' he's saying to me.

'No, never.' I allow myself a small smile. 'We-e-e-ll—maybe a few puffs at school once, when we were all trying to be daring.'

He smiles and nods as I go back to my declaration, and tick that yes, I have something to declare.

Then I fold up my table, get out my passport, and it's in the hands of the gods.

Jesus, Mary and Joseph. A perverse decision on my part, a memory of my Irish grandfather's favourite oath. A handful of coins each at the stall. All three looking grave, as if understanding what was going down. Jesus, like his dad, holding a carpenter's tool against his flowing cloak. I wonder if they made him make his own cross. Would he have chiselled and mortised the joints? Now that would be dying with dignity.

We descend and land and taxi into the unloading zone. I'm hot in my blue dress; it's sticking to my back. It's a wash and wear synthetic and I'm going to bundle it up and throw it in the garbage first thing when I get home. When I get home. I close my eyes and call up a vision of the kitchen, the smell of the lino, the chug of my ancient fridge. If all goes well, I can be there in a couple of hours. Just through customs, a short trip through the airport, past security, and into the taxi rank. I imagine pulling away in a cab, away from the airport and home free.

The thing to do now is forget about the cocaine, pretend I really am an innocent person. I keep my face demure as I watch the luggage turning on the silver conveyers. My case is an absolutely nondescript black. A luggage label in Spanish and English is tied carefully to the handle. Inside there are two changes of clothes, my toiletries and towel, a spare pair of shoes and three kilos of cocaine. Wonderful, splendid cocaine, meltingly pure and snowy. My superannuation fund brochure had outlined many exciting ways to spend your payment, but up your nose was not one of them.

I pick up the case. I carry it carefully to the customs declaration points and stand in a queue at the first gateway. I find that if I keep my mind on home and refuse to think about where I am, I can keep my heart rate down. Meditation, taken under sufferance at Dr Mick's urging, is proving to be an unexpected bonus. I meditate on the customs officer's hands as he takes my passport and declaration and notes things down, ticks boxes, glances into my face to check the likeness in the photo. His pen hesitates.

'Something to declare?'

'Yes.'

'Go to number seven at the end there. Thank you.'

Thank *you*. Gates one to six, green lights, are choked with people, children, luggage trolleys and bags. They will be hours. Number seven, a red light, has two people standing in it, both holding yellow plastic bags of duty-free and whatever else they think is declarable. As I move into place behind them, the first one sorts out his query with camera lenses and moves off. Through this gateway is the escalator, then the forecourt, then the self-opening doors to International Arrivals, then out onto the windy pavement of the airport and the taxis. God, God. Hold it together.

'I bought these lily bulbs in the airport in Hawaii,'

the punter in front of me is saying, 'and the girl said they're vacuum sealed and okay to take through without quarantine.'

'I'm afraid there's always someone who'll tell you that,' says the man in the uniform shortly. My heart rate, despite me, goes up a few notches. A closed face, an unhappy mouth, a stickler for the rules and in a bad mood to boot. 'They're illegal to import.'

'What do I have to do? Have them sprayed?'

'No, I'm afraid you have to surrender them to customs to dispose of.'

Down into the big chute they go. The passenger looks glum, but he's also through declarations in record time. I wonder if it was a deliberate ploy. His bags are searched in a rudimentary fashion. Cocaine is also surrendered to customs upon detection, and destroyed. Breaks your heart to think of it. All that brain-sharpening, energy-giving, nausea-suppressing potential chucked away.

I make my brain go somewhere else, focused anywhere rather than on the case in front of me. It has been my experience working with juvenile offenders that when they have stolen something their eyes keep swerving back to where they have hidden it. If it is secreted on their person they can't seem to stop their hands from going to that place. I look away, but there suddenly seems remarkably few places to look. My turn. Five minutes and I'm out. Five minutes. Jesus, Mary and Joseph.

'Good morning. Something to declare?' A deep breath. Hold body still, hold head still. Head-waggers are liars.

'Yes, I think so.' I reach over and snap open my own suitcase, and dig down the side. 'I thought I'd better check, better to be safe than sorry.'

I find the bottle and bring it out. He looks at it, noticing the seal, the liquid inside. He doesn't look surprised. Oh God, has this been tried before?

'It's holy water, you see. From the font at the Sisters of Mercy mission in Popayan.'

He checks my passport stamps. 'That's where you've just come from?'

'Yes, for the Semana Santa. I promised I'd try to get some for an ill friend. Does it have to be confiscated?'

He pauses, rubs his chin. 'Look, I'm afraid so. That water could contain all kinds of bacteria.'

'I just thought ... since it was sealed ...' I trail off. 'That's all right, I don't want to get you into trouble. I suppose the idea of water having healing properties seems quite ridiculous to you.'

He looks up briefly and gives me a quick, tired grin. 'Not at all, I'm a Catholic. Or was.' He reaches over and opens the suitcase. 'Is this your luggage?'

'Yes.'

'Did you pack it yourself?'

'I did, yes.'

'Are you aware of its contents?'

'Yes.'

He moves my clothes aside and takes out the three newspaper-wrapped packages. As he unrolls one I have a sense of standing looking at this scene as if through a long lens, the edges grey and prickling. When this happened when I was a child, it meant I was about to faint. Blue and white plaster appears, the face simpering with goodness. He raises his eyebrows enquiringly.

'It's a statuette of Our Lady, from the sisters at the convent,' I say. He holds it in his hand. I concentrate on the bottom of the statue for a moment, down by the foot where she's crushing the snake, down where the minutest crack can be seen in the plaster. It's smooth but not machine smooth, not solid cast. No, it's smoothed by hand, sitting on the floor of Emilia's kitchen with plaster mixed up in an old tin. Me having an attack of nerves and gabbling about taking it back, forgetting the whole thing, pissing off home. Emilia's low and sombre voice as she crouched there: *I took this risk for you, yeah? Now you take risk for yourself. It will work, you trust me. It will work.*

I can't drag my eyes away from that rough spot of plaster. Maybe it's an uncontrollable reflex after all. I look at the newspaper. The hands start wrapping the statue up again with quite careful deliberation, and he goes to unwrap the other two. Then hesitates. Oh Jesus, oh God, I promise with whatever time I have left I'll sing nothing but glory and praise to the short gift of my life, just please don't let him look too closely. I look at the coloured stamps on my passport, the ridiculous photo that Dr Mick had signed after a similar long silence of fervent prayer on my part and professional hesitation on his.

The customs guy smooths the newspaper and packs the statues carefully back in the case.

'I'm afraid I have to confiscate the water,' he says, his face grave.

I lower my eyes. 'Well, don't feel badly. I should have known you'd have to.'

He leans closer to me—God, another person about to betray an intimate confidence. 'You know what we sometimes do,' he says in a low voice. 'If the person's a really devout Catholic, say, and they've just made a lifetime trip to Lourdes, and the bottle's unsealed, then I say I just need to take the holy water into the quarantine office for a moment. Then I tip it into the disposal bin, and fill up the vial with ordinary water out of the tap, and take it back out to them. And they're as happy as Larry.'

He smiles again and I smile back, finding it easy now to look straight back into his eyes. 'Thank you for telling me that story,' I answer, 'because it doesn't matter a bit, you know, whether it comes from Lourdes or the tap. Because it's the faith that matters, the faith which heals. That's how you're blessed.'

He snaps my suitcase shut and turns it towards me, stamps my passport and hands it back.

'I'll let you get on your way then, Sister,' he says. 'Best of luck for the future.'

'Thanks,' I say, moving away towards the escalator and the doors out. There's a future out there all right, and once I get this outfit off I'm not going to miss one sweet open-mouthed breath of it. I am as light as a cloud as I walk towards the doors. I am free as air. I am blessed.

Flotsam

Out here there's a headwind, but they helped me drag a chair onto the verandah. A stupid chair, a white lounger with plastic webbing. It weighs next to nothing. Here the wind streams like liquid straight against my face.

I am smiling, inside the pouring hiss of wind. I expected change, certainly, but I thought that the place would have crumbled, as I have, by years of sting and salt. I never would have expected this gentrification, this odd new architecture of lime-washed palings and curlicues of wood, the weathervanes and lofts of American farmhouses. The shacks under their layer of pine needles gone without trace. The hotel's become lime-washed, too—all white in the dining room, polished boards revealed from under the carpet. The pub's nautical theme back in my day was twice-weekly fishermen's brawls, now it's gloss-painted; ceiling fans, brass fittings, mint-green trim. It's all polished up, sanded down, swept clean. I can't get used to it.

Out here the sea picks up the dark volcanic flecks and looks for something, sighs distractedly, turns them and searches. Small dark heaps of seaweed lie tangled at high-tide line, where the lip of the highest wave, draining away, has formed a long curving line of black. It's not very good sand. I went to pristine beaches later in my life where the sand squeaked, where it broke like a loaf of sugar. My feet were hard here, and crusted with mica and dark grains. The sea dipping in a sudden churning trough, a dangerous choppy pull, then you'd go out further and it would calm down.

Red needles up under the pines in the dark. Brushing them off your back. Matthew whispering, *Now you'll be for it.* A dusted salt rim on your legs, feet filthy. Don't know why I bothered going into the city to buy those shoes. A labour of love, my mother said, but that's what you did in those days. That's what you did.

Took them off after five dances because Matthew wanted to go outside and you didn't want to ruin them. Everything you owned was crusted with salt and mica. Pine needles and the smell of resin reminding you of your brother's violin. Resin, rosin, were they the same thing, you kept thinking, lying looking up through the pines, knowing that this was it now, actually happening, and all the wondering and unease that had come before had been like walking miles to buy the shoes.

The kids in the shacks sold bait to the drinkers in the hotel. *Look at your hair, you're like one of the shack kids*, your mother would say, or, *Look at your sister's runny nose, you'd think she lived in the shacks*. But when she was pregnant she pressed money into your hand and made you go down there and ask them for a bag of pippies, and she sat on the porch in her chair, feet flat and apart, belly huge, sucking the meat and salt water from the shells and looking out at the horizon but her eyes inward, focused on the task. As she bent down to get another pippy out of the bag she'd exhale, licking her lips. It was the sound Matthew made when he took the first sip of beer. The same craven absorption.

Can't we go for a walk, Lornie, let's just go for a stroll on the beach. Lornie, we can listen to a bloody pub singalong any time. There were big cracked bamboo chairs on this verandah then. Pinching your legs through the fabric of your dress. *Don't rip this, will you, Lornie, or you'll break my heart*, your mother had said, pinning the alteration under the waistband to her good dress from out of the trunk, refolding the crease with fingers suddenly deft and stroking. *This silk comes all the way from Siam.* Your younger sister watching silently from her homework on the kitchen table as your mother methodically stuck pins back into the pincushion. You, slim as a reed in the kitchen with shaved legs stinging, smelling the woody smell of Siam.

Come on, Lornie, don't be a spoilsport. I'll carry your shoes for ya. You've got to be home soon anyway.

Grey sea churning in the trough. There were teeth in there, gnawing at stones and shells. The sea moaned like a dog with a bone, licking it this way and that. Goosebumps on razor rash. Mustn't get this dress dirty. Up in the pines you step flinching on small sharp pine cones, and as you lie down it's a stupid thing but you're thinking of the violin again, the rosin dark and crackling on the bow, sifting into white powder as it strokes the strings.

Now you'll be for it. But you don't realise, with the house so busy with the new baby, your mother walking carefully up and down the front room as if she's the one barefoot on pine cones, wrapping the shawl around its head and singing a crooning, exhausted song, its livid scream like a seagull. Tiny hands pummelling that blue-veined breast as you try not to look. You don't realise until you're by the pier at low tide squatting down beside the rocks, smashing a pippy with a stone, saliva flooding your mouth and making your throat wince, picking out crushed shell and sand to gobble that meat. Rocking on your feet with the urgency.

They have glossy magazines here at the hotel now, on low tables made of bamboo lashed together. Smoked glass tops supporting those bubbly glass bottles, polished trochus and nautilus shells, and the magazines have perfume sachets inside, inviting me to experience some wholly new scent. *Are you sure there's nothing I can get you?* says the nice young girl who works here, leaning over me like a nurse. She wants me to come in. She wants to close the double glass doors against this wind—sand is getting onto the rugs, no doubt. From inside, you can look at the palm trees tossing and clacking, leaves streaming out like flags. They're looking threadbare now, these trees, like moth-eaten taxidermy exhibits, something in the worn-down section of the museum where nobody visits. *No, I'm fine here*, I tell her. I listen to the dog growl of the ocean, retrieving everything I throw in.

Why don't you wear that silk dress, Lornie? I don't know what's got into you, young lady. What's got into you is a nautilus, a starfish, a curled seahorse. Fingernails like tiny pink clear shells. Clamped onto the wall of you, and the suck and roar of your blood only making it cling more determinedly.

It's Matthew you're here to see on a grey Friday night, you can hear him there in the pub. The wind pushes clouds around, so that moon casts intermittent shadows. You lean against the palms and bend and snap pieces of frond, folding up lengths like concertinas. Breasts aching. He'll come out sooner or later to urinate in the back garden. *Don't say piss, girls, you sound like you were brought up in the shacks.* When he comes out you see he's drunk, coming down the grass like he's on board a pitching boat. When the men go out to catch herring they underplay the effect of the swell on them, holding casually onto the side, timing their movement. Drunk, they stagger and lurch and make more haphazard progress, unbuttoning their flies with owlish deliberation. Down on the sand you tell him and he shakes his head to clear it, looks back and sees you still there. You can see his mind shifting like a tide turning, draining backwards to leave everything looking untouched, saturated but untouched.

You better tell me all this tomorrow and we'll think about what we'll do to get rid of it, Lornie, you've caught me at a bad time here.

He slumps down next to you, hands over his face, hair in the sand. Next to you the sea pulls, searches, sighs. *Had a bit to drink tonight.*

Hiss and silence, hiss and silence. You hiccup your tears. After this, at home, there will be the ammonia smell of soaked hot nappies, a cot reeking of vomited milk.

Anyway, I'm out on the boat three days a week, how can I be sure it's mine?

Your blood sings. Sand under your digging fingernails, mica glittering even in the moonlight. You turn your scalded face to him, and he is unconscious. One hand rests lovingly, caressingly, on his belly.

Out there there's a trough, just where the water darkens and the surface ruffles like a sheet blowing on a line. Schools of tiny fish rock back and forth and there are shattered bits of kelp tumbling. In the trough, things go in rough and come out smooth, their edges worn away and polished. They are ground together and when the sea offers them back, nothing is sharp, nothing can cut.

You shake Matthew. He grunts and sleeps on. You are murderous, your mouth a black shadow of rage, sucking air in. You want to get a rock. Before you is a vision of smashed shell, drizzling water, grey salty tissue. You imagine that small sudden violence of skin tearing, blood, mucous, grit.

How easy it would be, now, to flood seawater through this, let the tide rinse everything clean.

You roll him into the water, towards the trough, and the sound coming from your mouth is a growl, a hiss. Once you saw a drowned man on this beach, returned searched and worried at by the sea. He lay like someone exhausted, resigned. A shining piece of ribbon kelp had twined itself around his neck, and his face had stopped resisting—welcoming the water in, welcoming the sand into a mouth at last relieved to be vulnerable. Matthew's body drifts easily into the shallows, unresisting. Soon waves will turn his face over and down. His lungs will breathe another element entirely.

You squat trying to rub grit from your legs for a long time before you realise it's not sand but regrowing hair. Only eight weeks ago you placed your foot on the chalky green rim of the bath and pulled the razor up in long strokes. Soap making the skin tight, blood trickling from a nick in your shin. Only eight weeks ago, it was your hipbones protruding through the fabric of the dress, your stomach that was flat.

You crouch, rocking, waiting for the sea to taste and take its gift.

In my room now, there's matting made of rope and a picture framed in weathered wood like old palings with the paint flaking off. How my mother would have laughed—or would she have wept?—to see these signs of poverty, which she worked to rise above, turned into this desirable high art. Perhaps these palings came from the shacks themselves, perhaps the collection of old bottles and driftwood fragments on the high shelf behind the bar came off one of those windowsills. I have no doubt they bulldozed the shacks, set a match to them. I can see the idle drinkers from the pub, standing outside and shifting their weight on the lawn, watching the orange flame and roiling black smoke, as clearly as if I witnessed it myself.

Not daring to put a foot on his neck, or kick him further into the trough. As you stand, you think you feel the thing in there fluttering and somersaulting, kicking and twisting. *Good*, you think. *You die, too*. And dig a fist in, praying for the ooze of warm blood and water, its salty mollusc slide down and away. *Die*. But it arches and bucks, tosses and hangs on. Breathes when you breathe. Clings and waits.

And God help you, you roll him out. Pull the body like a moonlit fish up over the tidemark. See seawater drizzle from his mouth, and soak into the sand. Dark hair plastered to a skull crowning like a keel onto a shore. A shuddering, hiccupping breath. A hand opening and closing, wonderingly, on the miracle of air.

I breathe in the new perfumes in their sachets, and their opulence makes me feel slightly sick. What an indecent amount I'm paying for this room here, when you think about it. I can see where they've knocked the wall down to give it these majestic proportions, my own balcony and clacking palms. When the salesmen stayed here back then, playing darts with the fishermen and chewing through platefuls of sausages and eggs, they probably paid less for a week than I'm paying each night. But money seemed to mean more in those days. It bought more.

My mother watched me coming up the path that night, the baby twisting and puking on her shoulder, and it must have been the way I walked. Or the way I stopped on the verandah and rested my hand on my hip. I've watched pregnant young women do it myself, before anything shows. It's the moment the idea has taken root, the shift in centre from the head to the belly, the careful movements. My mother watched me, her hand over her mouth, her eyes puffy from lack of sleep. As I stepped on the floorboards that didn't creak to catch the 6.00 a.m. bus, she was standing in the doorway and gave me her good purse that had been wrapped in tissue paper in the trunk with her money inside folded in a white hanky. As I took it she made a sound in her throat that I thought was out somewhere on the very edge of human, until my daughter was born, and I heard it again.

Where did that money come from, and what was it for? When my mother died my brother sent me some of her things, some embroidered linen and personal items packed in a box, and I imagined her making stitch after tiny stitch while we were at school, selling starched pieces to the women in the city. But it was not the thought of this that cut me most deeply, but her preserved wedding presents: the rolled white gloves, her empty 'Evening in Paris' perfume bottle, her foolish proud hope as she tucked the silk more perfectly into the waistband and smiled, getting up off her stiff knees with slow weary care. This, and the thought of whose escape the money was meant to buy.

My daughter wore the gloves one time, to a graduation party. Nineteen-twenties clothes were all the rage at the time and she and all her friends took photos of each other on the tiny front porch of my house in the city, each working the gloves up to her elbows and swooning across the doorway. My daughter's hands were slightly too big for those gloves. When she brought them home the next morning they were split along their fragile seams where her eager, careless fingers had forced them. Which is as it should be.

The first night I was here I requested a room at the back, facing the town. *The rattle of the palm trees kept me awake,* I said to the girl who's so pleasant, so accommodating. *Of course,* she said, humouring an old lady. They can't work me out, the staff. Their clientele are couples with late-model shining cars, who leave on Sunday night with rustic frames and squares of homemade soap from the craft shop, tied up with little bits of raffia twine. From the back-room window, I could look towards the main street. It's all restaurants and knick-knacks now, all baskets of painted flowerpots and doorstops and wind chimes as long as your arm which sound like distant church bells.

On the second day I walked past my own house. Children's bikes were slung around the front step and the hydrangeas needed cutting back. I had visualised myself walking up to the front door with a tidy little speech. I had imagined myself invited in by strangers who kept a respectful distance, stepping into that front room and turning the handle of the door into the bedroom, moving onto the flecked lino with the rag rugs, running my hand along the window sill. I imagined that if I opened the lid of the trunk that could not possibly still be there I would smell folded silk, dusty tulle of a yellowed wedding veil she let us wear occasionally for dress-ups, and the cologne scent of the Christmas tablecloth and matching napkins at the bottom. This was the scene I had plotted for myself, but when the moment came I just looked. I was conscious of myself, standing there at the gate, and the shape of my shadow bent up the path. An old woman. I walked on, trying to get as tired as I could, but still tossed and turned, dreaming of picking things up and putting them down again. When Monday came and the other guests left, I approached the girl again. *I've changed my mind,* I said. *I want to have a view of the sea after all.*

Over the wind and piles of seaweed, I can smell now that someone in the hotel kitchen is making an orange cake. I'll look like a wild woman with my hair blown about when I go in for afternoon tea. They think I'm dignified. Wealthy. A little mysterious. I grip the white arms of the plastic chair and breathe in, breathe out. The ocean rolls, yawns, tosses. There's that little line of dark objects thrown up on the sand, the brown trails of weed and crushed carapace, claw, broken purple and black mussel shells. Everything equally offered, everything its own kind of treasure, all exquisitely and abundantly wasted. Life story or death story, the tide still wrenches and smooths. Just wait, and the sea returns everything to you.

Cold Snap

When I go down to check my traps, I see the porch lights at that lady's place are still on, even though it's the morning now. *That's an atrocious waste of power*, my dad says when I tell him. His breath huffs in the air like he's smoking a cigar. The rabbit carcasses steam when we rip the skin off and it comes away like a glove.

Skin the rabbit—that's what my mum used to say when she pulled off my shirt and singlet for a bath. Mr Bailey gives me $3 for every rabbit to feed his dogs. I take them down in the wooden box with a picture of an apple on it. In the butcher's, rabbits are $2.50 but Mr Bailey says he likes mine better. I've got $58 saved. I want to get a bike.

Dad reckons it's good to save up your money. The tourists who stand around the real-estate agent's window looking serious, pointing, touching each other on the arm, he reckons they're loonies. When the lady up the road bought that house, my dad went over after the sold sign got stuck on and everybody had gone, and he took one of the palings off the side of the house and looked under at the stumps and made a noise like he was holding back a sneeze. *That lady's a bloody wacker*, my dad said. *Those stumps are bloody atrocious.*

He stood there looking at the house and rolled a cigarette. *Throwing good money after bad*, he said, and kicked the paling. I kicked it, too.

After she moved in I didn't set no more snares up there on the hill. I walked on the tracks round the lake, the tracks the rabbits make. I made myself small as a rabbit and moved through them on my soft scrabbly claws. I saw everything different then. Saw the places they sat and rested, the spots where they reached up with their soft noses and ate tiny strips of bark from the bottoms of the river willows. You've got to set a trap so that it kills the rabbit straight off. On the leg is no good. All night the rabbit will cry and twist, then you have to kill them in the morning when their eyes are looking at you, wondering why you did it. Mr Bailey, he tells me he can't believe I can catch them so near the town. I say you just have to watch things and work out where to put the trap, that's all. He nods so small you can only just see his chin moving up and down. *You've got it there, Billy*, he says.

After he gives me the money we look at the dogs and have a cup of tea. His dogs know me and why I come. Their eyes get different when they see me.

In the morning, everything is frozen. All up the hill are the trees, and every time I look at them I think of the time in school when I was right and Mr Fry was wrong. He showed us a picture and said trees lose their leaves in autumn and the other kids started writing it down but I felt the words come up, and I said they didn't, they lost their bark.

Mr Fry said how typical that the one time I'd opened my mouth in class I'd come up with a wrong answer. I looked at the trees standing bare in the mist and thought about how I'd kept shaking my head when he told me to say I was wrong, and the other kids sitting smiling, staring down at their hands, waiting for after school like the dogs wait for the rabbits.

When you smell the leaves, they're like cough lollies, and the bark goes all colours when it's wet. One day I was looking up at them and my eyes went funny and I flew up high and looked down at the tops of the trees all bunched together and they looked like the bumpy green material on the armchairs at my Aunty Lorna's place. I never told no one about that, not even my dad. The trees talk loud when it's windy and soft when it's quiet. I don't know what they talk about, probably about rain. When they get new gum tips, they're so full of sap they shiver in the air. Maybe they're excited. Or frightened.

But now that it's winter, the trees just look dark and sunken in, as if they're just hanging on by shutting off their minds, like my grandpop when he had the stroke and Dad said his body was just closing down slowly like something in the winter. And on the track, there's ice crystals on the clay, and when you look real close you can see the crystals are long, growing into lines, and the more mushy the clay the tighter the crystals pack in. They do it in the night, in the cold snap. You can put your foot at the edge of a puddle and just press real gently, and all these little cracks come into it, rushing outwards like tiny creeks.

Sometimes there's frost on the rabbits' fur. I brush it off with my hand. Rabbit fur smells nice, like lichen or dry moss. My mum left behind some leather gloves with rabbit fur inside, and when I put them on once I pulled my hot hands out and smelled her smell. *What are you bawling for?* my dad said. I hid the gloves just under my mattress. When I touch them they feel like a green leaf, just soft and dry and bendy and not knowing autumn's coming.

I looked up at the lady's porch lights the morning I got my new hat for my chilblains. Dad made it for me with rabbit skins. He rubbed my ears hard with his jumper and my mouth ached with holding it shut then he pulled the rabbit fur flaps down and tied them.

See you back here with the bunnies, he said, squeezing his hands under his arms before he stoked up the chip heater. One day a boy at my school who works at the feed supply told the other kids we were so backward we didn't even have hot and cold running water at our place. He said, *It's like Deliverance down there with you-know-who*. I asked Dad what deliverance was and he rolled a cigarette and said why. The next time he wanted chook pellets he asked for them to be delivered that day and then he stoked up the chip heater so high that a spray of boiling water gushed up and hit the roof like rain and it sounded like the fancy coffee machine at the milk bar. When this boy came around with the pellets, Dad told him to empty them into the bin and then said would he like to wash the dust off his hands in the kitchen. The boy went in. I stood looking at the chooks and made myself small like them and felt the straw under my claws as I scratched around, and felt how the wheat powdered as I cracked it in my beak, and then there was a scream and the boy came running outside holding his hands out in front of him. And they were bright pink like plastic. As the boy ran past, my dad called, *Don't forget to tell your friends.*

I pushed the rabbits into a hessian bag and heard music coming out of the house with the lights on. It was violin stuff. I saw the lady who'd bought the house come out onto her porch as I cut across the ridge. She was wearing King Gees and you could see the new fold marks in them. She had hair the colour of a fox. When she saw me her face went all bright and excited even though she didn't know me, like the lady doctor who did all those stupid tests on me at school just saying stupid words and expecting me to make up more words and say them straight away and not giving me any time to think it over.

She said, *Well, hello there, has the cat got your tongue?* She had lipstick on. I thought maybe she was on her way to church.

I said I didn't have a cat and her eyebrows went up.

You're up very early on this wintry morning. What's that you've got in your bag? she said, like we were going to play a joke on someone. I showed her the top rabbit's head and her mouth went funny and she said, *Oh dear, oh the poor little things. What did you want to kill them for?*

I said for Mr Bailey. I said they died very quickly and always got the traps right around their necks. She hugged herself with her arms and shook her head and said goodness me, looking at my rabbit-skin hat. I turned my head slowly round so she could see better.

She asked me suddenly if I lived in the house down the hill and I said yes. Then she said what a marvellous location and what a shame the power would cost an arm and a leg to put through, otherwise she would have made an offer, and that this little place she'd picked up was such fun and a goldmine. She said all her friends from the city thought she was quite mad but she'd be the one laughing when property values went up and she'd done all the extensions. I was waiting for her to finish so I could go. I could feel the rabbits stiffening up inside their bag; I could smell them.

What's your name? she asked me finally and I said Billy.

And do you go to school, Billy?

I looked at her and said you have to. Her eyes went all crinkly and happy again.

And is it a special school, just for special children?

I couldn't work her out. Maybe she didn't understand about school. I said not really then my mouth blurted out: *You got hair like a fox.*

She laughed like someone in a movie. *Good heavens*, she said. *You are a character, aren't you?*

A man in a red dressing-gown came out onto the verandah and the lady said, *Look darling, some local colour.*

Love the hat, said the man to me. I waited for them to tell me their names, but the man just complained that it was bloody freezing, and thank Christ they'd got the central heating in. The lady said yes, the whole place was shaping up well, then she looked out down the track and said, *The only problem is there's no bloody view of the lake.* Then she said, *Billy, show Roger your bunnies, darling*, and I pulled one out and Roger said, *Good God.*

They both laughed and laughed and Roger said, *Well it looks like the light's on but there's no one home.* Which was wrong. They were both there and they'd turned the light off by now.

When I walked down the track past the sharp turn and through the cutting my boots cracked on the black ice. You can easy go for a sixer on that. People say it's invisible but it's not really. You have to get down real close to see where the water's froze then melted a bit then froze again, all through the night, till it's like a piece of glass from an old bottle.

Dad had had his shower by the time I got home. The rabbits were harder to skin because more time had passed. The skins ripped off with the sound of a bandaid like they put on your knees in the school sickroom. *Get them off*, my dad said when I came home one time with the bandaids on. He was watching me so I pulled both of them off fast and they bled again. *Call that first aid? That's bloody atrocious*, said my dad. *Get some air onto them.* I looked at my knees. They felt like the hinges inside had got stiff and rusty, like the oil in them had leaked out.

Every day for the next few weeks, people drove up the hill to fix things in the house. You could hear banging and machines and then a pointy bit of new roof pushed up over the trees. The lady's friends, the ones who thought she was quite mad, came up a lot at first but then it got colder and they stopped. The lake froze over at the edges and the ducks had frost on their feathers. One day I crept up and saw the lady standing with her arms folded on the new verandah, which was covered in pink paint, just staring out at the trees. All around her garden were piles of rocks and I saw a duck standing still as anything under a tree. I went closer and she saw me.

Well, Billy, she called, and I went over and saw the duck was a pretend one.

Look at all these bloody trees, she said, sighing. *I'm sick of the sight of them.*

She had on the overalls again but they didn't look so new now. The digger had left big piles of dirt everywhere.

What are *those trees anyway, Billy?* she said suddenly, and I said they were gum trees and she laughed and said she might have guessed that would be my answer, even though I hadn't finished and was only sorting out what I was going to say next.

I said it was going to be another cold snap that night and more hard weather. And she said how did I know and I started explaining but she wasn't really listening, she was still looking down the gully towards the lake, turning her head like the ladies in the shop when they're buying dresses and looking at themselves in the mirror, deciding.

Three weeks after that time I was up in the trees, just listening to them and looking for good spots for snares, when I found the first sick one. When I touched its leaves I knew it was dying, like when I touched my grandpop's hand. It was a big old tree and used to have a big voice but now it was just breathing out. And it was bleeding. All around the trunk there was a circle somebody had cut and sap dripped out which is the tree's blood, my dad says. It was a rough chopping job and the person had used a little saw then a hatchet and I could see how they didn't know how to use the saw properly and had scratched all up and down around the cut. There was nothing I could do for that tree. I wanted to kill it properly so it wouldn't just stand there looking at me trying its hardest to stay alive.

The week after that one I found another tree that was the same and then it just kept on happening, seven of the biggest trees got cut. When I looked real hard I flew up again and saw them from the top and the dying ones made a kind of line down to the lake all the way from the lady's house on the hill to the shore. Then I came back down onto the ground, and I saw how it was.

You've done it again, Billy, said Mr Bailey when I came past. *I don't know what I'd do without you, two big fat ones today.*

I got my money and walked up the hill towards the lady's house and I saw her through the trees planting something in the garden. Dad said she kept the whole nursery in business.

Now I got quite close to her and the pretend duck before she saw me and she jumped backwards.

Jesus, kid, just give it a break, will you? she said in an angry voice. I stood there holding the empty box from the rabbits.

Just don't creep around so much, Billy, okay? she said, getting up. I saw she had a special little cushion for kneeling on and I was looking at that cushion when she said something else.

Where did you get that box, Billy?

I said out of the shed. She laughed and looked up at the sky. I looked down at the box with the picture of the apple on it.

Out of your shed? That's a finger-joint colonial box, Billy. Do you know how much some of them are worth?

Her voice was all excited, like that lady at the school who pretended boring things were interesting on that test.

What about selling it to me, she said.

I said it was my rabbit box and she said did I have any others in the shed. I said I would have a look. She was a loony. My dad sometimes split up old boxes for the chip heater. He kept nails and bolts in them.

I know where there'll be a lot, I said. *At the Franklin's garage sale.*

Her eyes looked a little bit like Mr Bailey's dogs' eyes inside the netting.

When is it? she asked.

On Sunday. They got lots of stuff.

Like what? she said, and then said a whole list of things like *fire pokers? ironwork? cupboards?* and I just kept nodding.

Lots of that kind of thing, I said. *Lots of these little boxes with writing and maps of Australia and animals like emus.*

She folded her arms and looked at me harder. *Boxes with emus and kangaroos on them? With joints like this one?*

Yep, I said, *but you got to get there real early in the morning. Like 6.30 or something. 'Cos other people come up from the city.*

She asked me where Franklin's was, and I told her.

I can get there earlier than the dealers, she said, looking down the hill at the row of trees, all secretly dying.

On Saturday I set a snare just inside a little tunnel of grass by the lake. Dad says it's bad to kill something without a good reason but I knew the rabbit wouldn't mind. The trees were very quiet now. It was going to be a black frost. When the moon came up there was a yellow ring around it like around a Tilley lamp when you take it out on a frosty night.

I couldn't hardly get to sleep with thinking. I thought of her going out there with her new saw from the hardware shop and cutting open their skin. In the night, while the rabbits nosed around with their soft whiskery mouths and Mr Bailey's dogs cried and choked on their chains over and over.

When I got up it was still dark, as dark as the steel on the monkey bars, cold metal that hurts your chest. I felt a still, cold rabbit's body in the trap and I felt sorry for it. I knew she would, too. Because in the lady's head you can feel sorry and worried for rabbits but not for trees.

It looked like it was sitting up there by itself on the track, alive. All the crystals had grown in the night and now the black ice was smooth as glass all round that turn.

I got back into bed when I was finished. I felt my mum's gloves.

My dad knew I'd got up early when he came to wake me up again. I don't know how.

You'd better go out and check your traps, he said as he split the kindling.

Up the road Farrelly's tractor was pulling her car out of the ditch. It had crumpled into one of the big gums, and leaves and sticks had been shaken all over it. Mr Farrelly said the ambulance blokes had nearly skidded over themselves on the bloody ice, trying to get in to help. *What's a sheila like her doing getting up in the bloody dark on a Sunday morning anyway*, Mr Farrelly said as he put the hooks on. *Bloody loonies.*

Under the front wheel I saw white fur, turned inside out like a glove, like my hat. I went down through the trees, touching the sick ones. On the way I stepped in a big patch of nettles. No use crying if you weren't looking out for yourself, my dad says. I looked around and found some dock and rubbed it on and it stopped hurting like magic. That's what nature's like, for everything poisonous there's something nearby to cure it if you just look around. That's what my dad says.

I made a little fire and smoked my traps. Five more weeks and I can get a mountain bike.

Resize

The car breaks down on the way to the jeweller's. It hits a pothole filled with mud the colour of strong tea and Dave hears the fanbelt snap and clatter under the bonnet like the end of a spool of film. This is in his mind so that when he gets out he sees the whole scene like a kind of movie — black and white, bittersweet, European. Something on SBS. He makes an expressive Gallic face at the radiator and feels the rain drizzle down his collar.

'So what's the story?' Andrea shouts with her head out the window. 'I thought you fixed the bloody thing. I thought you said this would never happen again.' Behind the fogged windscreen, her face settles back into hard, sceptical lines of resignation. In the movie, she is the unforgiving French girlfriend, cool and intimidating. He lays the flat of his hand against the radiator cap, feeling heat, turning it and wary about the pressure release of boiling spray. What he'd fixed had been the timing chain.

'It's freezing. How could it boil on a day like this? Bastard car.' She slouches back against the red bench seat, a ridge of thumbnail is excised by her teeth in small, annoyed nips. She hates the Holden. He feels protective of it when he sees it parked on the street, as if it were an old dog: smelly and incontinent, losing dignity, but *his*.

Andrea twists the ring on her finger, massaging circulation back in distractedly. They are going to have their wedding rings cut off and resized. Dave's cuts into his finger with a sharp, blackened niggling; Andrea's flesh rises up either side of her ring like bread dough left to prove too long. They can't get them off. It has happened to both of them at the same time, like an anniversary.

The jeweller is a friend of Andrea's and has agreed to cut the rings off at his house and add another section of gold. They are late. The jeweller lives in a mud-brick house at the end of eight kilometres of dirt track.

Dave searches the boot for a spare fanbelt. He shifts a roll of carpet underlay Andrea has picked up off a skip for controlling weeds and a bag of chook pellets, feeling the rain saturate his back. His ring finger itches and burns around the cut on his knuckle where he tried this morning to lever the ring off with soap and a crochet hook.

He swears as he shifts stuff around, feels the edge of his underpants get wet just as Andrea's left hand comes out the window holding the new fanbelt as if it were four aces. Of course—the glovebox. In the SBS movie, Dave thinks grimly, this would be a fairly comical image. He changes the belt, tops up the water, and gets back in the car, wiping his hands on an old T-shirt and feeling his wet clothes paste themselves to him.

He blows his nose and looks sideways at his wife chewing the inside of her lip, and after a moment she looks back at him.

'Let's just get this over with,' she says in the long-suffering tone that annoys the crap out of him.

Andrea has had a dream the night before that her friend the jeweller had a tiny circular saw and started cutting through the gold band, then kept going and went right through skin and bone and gristle, cutting off her whole finger. Best to amputate, he'd said, flattening the rest of her hand out on a kind of operating table. Fine, she'd thought in the morning. Whatever.

Dave pumps the accelerator, double-clutches to find first. The Holden's shift column protests. It's like a metal grinder in there. Andrea jammed it between first and second once and he'd fixed it with a hammer, explaining to her about the slipping clutch until she'd suddenly leaned on the horn and he'd cracked the back of his head on the bonnet.

'A slipping clutch,' she'd said when he'd got back in, a strainer-wire of tension between them. Her voice had been heavy with sarcasm, and something else. 'Yeah, right.' And she'd smirked—a private joke with herself she didn't think he'd get.

He'd driven the car on their first date. She'd liked it then, said it was like being in an ad, an old romantic 1950s ad, searched the dial on the big, old radio for something atmospheric. He was in awe of her. There was no bullshit about Andrea. She wore those op-shop dresses with aplomb, bossed people round when they wouldn't give her student concession. Making love in the back, his first euphoric inhalations of her had swirled with old leather, petrol, oily rags. Herbal shampoo. He inhales now—nothing but wet jumper.

Down the dirt track it's like Andrea blames him personally for every rut, as if he's providing suspension with his own body. Dave winces, thinks of the time he pranged the car and felt something in the driveshaft crack with a terrible finality, like a spine.

It's welded back together now. Patchily.

Andrea's gearing up for some tight-lipped blame, but the jeweller's forgotten they were coming anyway. Her marshalled energy hangs awkwardly in the calm. The jeweller makes coffee, and to cut the rings off they sit at a work table slung with an apron of leather. In the leather, Dave sees a dust, a sifting of gold specks and filings. A deep, exhausting sadness fills him. He can't explain it; it's the filings and Andrea's proferred finger, swollen with the ring's confinement, the others so fine and tapered. The jeweller holds her hand as he cuts as if he's fashioned it himself, as familiar as a lover.

'Thank God for that,' Andrea says, flexing. Dave's cut burns as his ring gets filed off; the relief and release are draining. He sifts through the gold filings and they powder his fingers. He compares this table with their own, a wedding present from a carpenter friend seven years ago, littered with bills and notes and lists, a bowl of brown-flecked bananas, cups rimmed with tidemarks of coffee.

Andrea is talking to the jeweller as she never talks to him; he hears news and opinions from her he wasn't aware of. At home she sits mired in long bouts of silence, sometimes glaring at the TV with something else, some other narrative entirely, racing away behind her eyes. He's given up trying to find out what; he's sick to death of being cast as the one meant to guess.

Dave follows the conversation now, baffled, hearing only enthusiasm and laughter. He stares at the tiny files and awls on the workbench. A screwdriver with an end no larger than a needle, some microscopic precision-clamping device that looks like it could clench together two single synapses in the human brain. Dave listens to his wife's vivacity and the jeweller coming awake under her wit and energy, listens to the movie unspooling. He's missed a connection somewhere, he thinks, some subplot, some richer underlying symbol that would throw light on the whole. With a sort of horror he realises he's close to tears and turns and stares out the window, feels himself floundering, fighting off a heavy pointlessness with revulsion, as if it were a jellyfish or a piece of looming dead flotsam.

The jeweller finds a device bored with holes of different sizes and Dave and Andrea both push their ring fingers through. As they stand—the jeweller jotting down a figure and explaining how he will rejoin the rings and repolish the surfaces—Dave finds he has to stare out the window again. Their hands are so close, making room for each other, not touching. He feels numb.

As they are leaving, Andrea puts her hand on his arm and mechanically he gets out his wallet.

'Oh, pay me when you come and pick them up,' says the jeweller. The moment stumbles, then rebalances. Andrea looks at Dave. She has only meant to touch him, he realises, not command obedience. It makes him catch sight of himself, shake himself awake. There is recognition in her eyes, shame, a stricken glimpse of something emptied, a gulf of ragged edges and constriction.

'Sorry,' she says.

He feels the moment heat up, become molten.

Andrea struggles with the car door, gets in and manoeuvres it closed, for once not swearing at it. The jeweller disappears back inside; his garden blurs and runs through the streaming windscreen.

The heat is in Dave's chest now. They sit there, breathing. He knows as soon as he starts the car there will be a cooling again, a loss of this strange fluidity, so he floats in it, feeling it rearrange him, before turning to look at his wife.

There is her, and there is everything after this; her transforming face, her naked fingers, her precise choreography. He can no sooner think of not having her as pulling a layer out from under his own skin.

She leans over and kisses him on the mouth, pulls back

and grins. The heat spreads, stretches. He fears for a moment the join may not hold. There aren't tools small enough for this. There aren't subtitles.

'How's the swelling?' he croaks. On her cheek there's a glitter of metal where his fingers must have brushed her. He can smell her hair.

'Going down,' she says.

He steps on the clutch and finds first gear, feeling the calibrations gnash like teeth momentarily then drop into place, lubricated, fitted together like bones in a hand.

The Testosterone Club

I have left my husband: rolled up my wedding linen around my wedding crockery, packed it all into the back of my car wedged safely with my wedding towel set, and left.

Six years is a long time—especially, as the old joke goes, when you consider you only get four for armed robbery—and the crockery is by no means a complete set any more. It stands testament to the chips and dings and cracks of a careless and imperfect marriage, but I have tucked it in gently around my preserving kit on the back seat. The preserving kit is in pristine condition—perfectly preserved, you might say, if you were in the mood for making jokes. I valued it highly, when I was married. Yesterday.

Other households greet spring and summer because the flowers come out and lambs gambol and butterflies dance in the meadow; my husband welcomed spring because it meant I could buy boxes of vegetables at knockdown prices and start preserving. Pickled cucumbers and onions were a particular favourite, preferably ingested slowly in front of *Saturday Sporting World.*

My husband didn't excel at any one sport; he watched them all equally. He could work his way through a jar of pickled onions in an afternoon. It's thirsty work, and several beers were required, forming a lethal cocktail of yeast and vinegar. He had two mates who were unfailing in their support of this. They would arrive on Saturday at 12.15, just in time for lunch, then settle into watching the match. Actually it's unfair to say they only watched — their participation in the game fell just short of actually playing it. They yelled, they writhed, they spear-tackled each other across the couch and slid crunchingly over the rug, rising with faces of serious concentration and pieces of corn chip clinging to their hair. They even dressed the part, in tracksuits and expensive running shoes. Their hair was damp and tousled as if they'd just stepped from the shower in the gym; they carried with them a misleading but unmistakable hint of liniment. Macka, Chooka and my husband, Barry. Or Barra, as he was known. They were a club. A testosterone club.

I made up this name myself. It wasn't so much because of their adoration of sports and each other, the aggressive pawing as one would playfully spring the other in a headlock. It was more to do with their complete confidence in their own majestic sexual magnetism. They woke in the morning with this confidence; it accompanied them into every sphere they stepped, assured and unshakable. Together, they entered a room pelvis-first; it made them sit with legs stretched wide apart to accommodate their mythic proportions, so much so that fitting on the couch together was often tricky. It made them offer me a drink with burly protectiveness as they pulled their own from the fridge and noticed me working in the kitchen, preparing snacks for the third quarter. It made Barry look at me with beery pride when I came in, like I was something he'd won unexpectedly in a raffle.

One of these club members I was married to, which was worrying enough. But it was from Macka and Chooka that the hormone in question truly asserted itself.

One Saturday, Macka entered the kitchen and watched me for a few moments at the bench. I was peeling onions and could feel his eyes on me, sizing me up.

'Everything okay, Macka?' I said finally.

'Yeah, sure, sweet. Everything okay with you?'

I glanced up and nodded. He strolled around the counter.

'No, I mean, everything okay with you and Barra?' he said meaningfully.

'Sure. It's the onions, Macka.'

'Yeah, yeah. Just wondering, you know, because he's a top bloke, and well … you're'—he fiddled with the ring-pull on his can—'you're really nice,' he finished.

I wiped my eyes with the back of my hand. 'Well, thanks, Macka.'

'And if you ever need anything, Monica, you know who you can call. You know what I mean?'

His eyes were boring into me under his brows—well, brow, really.

'Well, yeah, I think I know what you mean. Thanks,' I said, tears streaming down my face. I turned and stepped into the pantry for something when I was overwhelmed by a cloud of liniment. Macka was behind me. A millimetre behind me, and closing fast on the inside flank.

'I knew it,' he whispered, enfolding me in his arms but careful not to spill his beer. For a second or so I was too stunned to move.

'Get off me,' I said, blinking still from the onions.

'I always knew you liked me,' he was saying.

'I mean it.' I broke his grasp and wrestled free. 'Don't be ridiculous.'

He smiled, cocked his head towards the living room and nodded. 'I get ya,' he said. 'Some other time, eh? You give me a ring.' He strolled back to the television, chewing a handful of peanuts.

And I let it go—call me an idiot, but I did. I had a chance to bring it up the following evening, when Barry and I were lounging on the couch watching the Sunday night movie, full of fruit-and-nut chocolate and cosy bonhomie.

Hey, Barry, I could have said, snuggling up to him, *have a guess what Macka said to me yesterday. Can you believe it?* I could have tried for a tone of affectionate amusement. I tried the approach on for size, staring at the TV, then left it unsaid. The moment passed.

I was hanging out the washing the following Friday when Chooka strolled into the backyard.

'Hi,' I said with a smile, struggling with a sheet. 'What

are you off work so early for?'

'Let me give you a hand with that,' Chooka said, reaching up and straightening the sheet uncertainly. He stared at the pegs like Marco Polo first glimpsing chopsticks, then selected a singlet and arranged it carefully next to the sheet. I smiled encouragingly.

'Thanks a lot. Want a cup of coffee?'

'Yeah, okay. Barry not home?'

I looked at him. Chooka knew Barry's schedule better than I did.

'No—why? Should he be?'

He laughed, a gurgling, strained laugh. 'Just wondered.'

'Haven't you guys got plans to go to the club tonight?'

I was inside by now, plugging in the kettle, reaching for the biscuits, watching Chooka as he strolled around the kitchen, toying with the eggtimer.

'Yep. We're meeting down there at 7.00. I just got off work early and thought ... I'd come and pay you a visit.'

'That's nice.' There was a pause that couldn't be called anything but awkward as we both listened to the kettle reach boiling point then turn itself off.

'That kettle going alright, is it?' Chooka said suddenly, and I remembered he had given it to us as a wedding gift.

'Yes, yes, it's great. Use it every day.'

We sat on the couch. As I sipped my coffee a sweaty hand landed across my shoulders.

'So how you doing then?' Chooka said, giving my shoulder an affectionate squeeze.

'Good ... thanks.'

'You must get a bit lonely here by yourself of a day, eh Monica?' As he spoke, his hand moved down the space between my arm and my side, the fingers wriggling. A grope. Or, in Chooka's books, single-step foreplay.

'Cut it out, Chooka.'

'Just bein' friendly.' He gave a ghastly grin, then put his cup on the table and grabbed my hand teasingly.

'Yeah, well ...' I began, then my hand was deposited on his groin, and held there. I yelped, trying not to spill my scalding coffee in his crotch. Again, I was speechless. After all, first Macka and now Chooka—was it something I'd said? I pulled my hand free and very deliberately wiped it on my jeans.

'I think you should leave,' I said.

'You won't tell Barry about this, will ya?' he said as he stood, at a loss. Rejection hadn't occurred to him; the script was written and directed by testosterone.

'I might.'

'Well, I wouldn't. Whatever's gone on between you and me, Monica, that's private, okay? Barry doesn't need to know about this.'

He stalked out before what romance novels call his visible male hardness could return to its normal dimensions. I sat there, winded. Now what? As I emptied the dishwasher and washed Chooka's mug, I wondered how I was going to break this to Barry. Again, I had my chance. He came home with a box full of jars the cleaner at work had given him, ready for sterilising for home preserves. On the way he'd stopped off and bought a half-case of vinegar and kilos of mustard seeds, ready for the weekend markets. He'd even bought me a new book, *The Home Preserver: Everything You Need To Know About Putting Food By*. On the cover was a woman in a frilled apron, who had the simpering, scrubbed look of a fundamentalist sect member, gazing adoringly at a line of neatly labelled jars. Barry seemed filled with an almost evangelical fervour as he glanced through the pages.

'See, look at this, Monica. Snap and colour, that's what the experts say. That's what you should be striving for. So we need to get cucumbers no bigger than that, okay?' He held up a thumb and forefinger. I looked and nodded. These would not be mere baby cucumbers, these were to be premature cucumbers, snatched from the vine before full term, plunged into the humidity crib of the sterilised jar. I nodded, while in my mind sang the sentence that had been hanging there immobile: *Hey, guess what happened this afternoon, Barry? Your mate Chooka put the hard word on me. Macka tried the same thing last Saturday. That makes both of your mates, Barry.* I stared dreamily at the gap he was emphasising, letting his words drift over me.

'Got it, Mon?' he was saying.

'Sure,' I said with a bright smile.

The next day it was footy as usual — hot dogs and mustard, stubbies of beer and lots of shouting. Macka and Chooka didn't meet my eye much. At half-time they made a pretence of watching the cheer squad march onto the ground and do high kicks in the drizzle. The three of them went out to the club that evening and I was idly watching an old video when Barry returned. I heard the front door slam and Barry thumped into the bathroom. He re-emerged five minutes later, storming through the kitchen swing doors like Wyatt Earp into a saloon, only in a short white towelling dressing gown decorated with his initials.

'Something wrong?' I said.

'Bloody oath there's something wrong. I got a nasty surprise tonight, Monica, a very nasty surprise.' I looked enquiring. The parking ticket in the glove box? But no.

'When a bloke can't trust his own wife, Monica, there's gotta be something seriously wrong.'

'I'm sorry?'

'First Macca tells me while we're having a game of pool, then blow me if Chooka doesn't have the same thing to say while we're putting a few dollars through the poker machines.'

I made my face go blank. 'Tell you what?'

His eyes flashed. 'Don't pretend you don't know. About you. You propositioning them.'

'What?' I made the mistake of letting an incredulous laugh escape me, and sat up on the couch. 'Listen to me, Barry. Your mates were the ones that came on to me, and did it with all their Neanderthal allure, let me tell you. And now that I've been nice about it and haven't embarrassed them ...'

'Are you trying to tell me my best mates propositioned you?' There was a high note of disbelief in his tone.

'Barry, use your brain for a moment and tell me which seems more likely to you. I mean really. Think about it.'

I could hear his teeth grinding. And his brain. 'When, then?'

'Friday and last Saturday.'

'Then why didn't you tell me?'

I laughed again, bitterly, slumping back helplessly on the scatter cushions. 'Because it just seemed so ridiculous. And I thought you'd be embarrassed, too.' I threw a cushion at him. 'And because I made the mistake of thinking they'd maybe want to forget all about it, if you want the truth. But I should have known better, I guess.'

Good old Barry. There he stood, the man who wore a ring that matched mine, who slept next to me every night, who was at this very minute weighing up my word against that of his two drinking buddies. It was me against the testosterone club. But Barry, I told myself, Barry was the man I was married to. Surely Barry couldn't be that dumb.

'Don't bullshit *me*, Monica,' said my husband.

Snap and colour. Barry was as insistent about it as he was about them being no bigger than that. Pickled cucumbers made at home can occasionally go greyish and flabby. You will have noticed how well commercial pickles take lurid food dyes — Barry wasn't having any of that. After three days of stony, wounded silence, he brought home a box of chocolates and a much larger one of very small vegetables, led me to the chapter in *The Home Preserver* about old-fashioned ways to keep snap and colour, and left me to it. I could sense this was my test, my chance for redemption. I bowed my head and read it humbly.

Basically, you add a preserving agent in powder form. My grandmother used to keep some of the powders listed to retain snap and colour in her laundry cupboard. I recognised one she used to put on her hydrangeas, one she applied in a pinch to mouth ulcers, even one, I think, that she used to make her own mothballs. This alarmed me. Surely you shouldn't eat tincture of iodine sulphate?

I went to the library, in the interests of the perfect cucumber pickle, and asked for a reference book on chemical compounds — can you believe how conscientious I was? — and waited while they dithered around getting one with fragile, rice-papery pages from out of the archives. I dragged this book over to a window seat and looked up the effects of the chemical agent, 'available at any reputable chemist or apothecary', which the cookbook had recommended for pickling.

I sat back, surprised. Then read it again. I looked at the date of the reference book —1879.

Used in cases of excitability, said the book, *initially stimulates gastro-colic reflex, direct enervating and cumulative effect on male's production of testosterone, decreases vigour over long period of application, useful in hysteria.*

Snap and colour, Barry? I thought as I gazed out the window. *You shall have them.* I returned the book and went to a reputable apothecary.

The Home Preserver, I hasten to add, was quite clear in its application. Per quart of liquid (American measurement) you are meant to add the merest pinch, a half of a flattened teaspoon, to achieve the pickle of your dreams. This, they point out, reacts with the acetic acid in your herbed vinegar to prevent that rubbery effect that can so easily spoil a good cucumber. And I had the teaspoon ready, I honestly did. But I was listening to Macka and Chooka and Barry hooting and crashing in the living room, horsing around in their tracksuits and liniment, and I suddenly thought, *Well, who the hell knows what a quart is anyhow?* And my hand sort of ... slipped.

Calm down. It's not going to kill anybody. But it's interesting, isn't it—ironic even, when you consider its long-term effect—that a chemical which does so much to keep cucumbers firm and non-flaccid has quite the opposite effect on the male organ. It doesn't occur suddenly, the book had said, and you'd no doubt need to injest a fair amount over a period of time before you started noticing any changes, but wilt it will. Oh, yes. You'll be looking at that space between thumb and forefinger in a whole new light.

I watched the powder dissolving into the vinegar and drifting around the cucumbers, smiling to myself because it reminded me of one of those kid's souvenirs where snow falls in a little dome on some little landscape; a desert island, say, or—in this case more appropriately—the Big Banana. I shook a jar. The cucumbers, warty and ghostly in their vinegar formaldehyde, bobbed around like specimens. This many pickles were going to take months and months to eat. And suddenly I realised I had no intention of being there.

Barry, after seeing my defection as an admission of guilt, will hold me no conscious grudge—I've left him and the boys a huge supply to be going on with. It'll take them an entire football season to get through what's left, marinating gently in their dill-flavoured broth. I was generous with the herbs and spices. I was unstinting.

I hum a tune to myself as I pull out of the driveway, hearing the china clink in the back as I hit the tarmac. It'll be weeks, probably, before any of them notices anything a little ... amiss. But never, never, never would they mention it to each other. And I doubt they'll think to change their diets. Nothing like a crunchy, firm, green cucumber pickle, thrusting proudly up from your fingers, no bigger than that. Perhaps with a little cheese, a few dry biscuits, a celery stick. I have left the jars in the fridge, lined up as impressively as show exhibits. Pickled cucumbers, dill cucumbers, pickled onions, artichokes, vegetable medley, baby beetroot. Always have them chilled and crisp, advises *The Home Preserver*, and I tend to agree.

They are a delicacy. How shall I put this ...? They are a dish best served cold.

Dark Roots

You'll be fitting your key in the lock when you hear the phone start ringing, and straight away your hand will be fumbling with haste. The answering machine will kick in and when your heart squirms up around your throat somewhere, you'll know. Call it what you like, we think it's love, but it's chemical. It's endorphins, that high-octane fuel, revving the engine and drowning out the faint carburettor warning sound in the back of the head, the out-of tune chug that says *wait, wait,* in its prim, irritating little voice.

At the doctor's, you'll keep your eyes on the package of contraceptive pills made into a desk paperweight. Your doctor will look over your card, tapping a pen, then reach for the prescription pad, and ask you if you've been on these before.

'Oh, many years ago now,' you say.

'Any side-effects?'

You remember being twenty-two, going on the pill for the first time, and lock onto the memory of your own body in a swooping rush. You remember your long thighs in those slimline jeans, and your flat stomach which effortlessly stayed that way, hard with muscles you'd done nothing to deserve. You remember — and what woman over thirty-five doesn't? — pulling your long hair up over a sun visor and sitting on beaches with boyfriends for hours, squinting into the glaring, ruinous sun, glorifying in being tanned.

'No side-effects that I can remember,' you say. 'Maybe an increased appetite.'

The doctor smiles briefly. 'Yeah, they'll give you the munchies all right, you'll have to watch that. You're not a smoker, are you?'

'No.'

'Only because if you were, at your age, I'd never be prescribing this brand.'

And you feel that little swoop again, hear the *at your age* like stepping on a sharp piece of gravel, a wince of ludicrous defensiveness.

It's the same when you break the news to your friends.

'Come on then,' they say. 'No one *cares*, Mel. Just tell us how much younger the guy is.'

'Thirteen years,' you answer. You want — no, you *need* — one of them to come in on cue now, with something sisterly about nobody even *commenting* on the difference if it was the other way round. Instead there is a surprised silence. Come on, somebody.

'Well,' says Helen abruptly, 'I mean, for godsakes. If he

was thirty-nine and you were thirteen years younger nobody would turn a hair. I say go for it.'

You will crush the lemon slice in your drink with the edge of your straw. You need more.

'I mean, look at you, you're gorgeous. No wonder,' says Sandy. 'I bet the guy can't believe his luck. What is it you said he did?'

You wonder, later, why you lie here. Why you say Paul is an academic, even though he's actually just finishing his PhD and tutoring. Why you have to add: 'And he writes movie reviews.'

Then later, standing in your bathroom, about to perforate the foil package and take that first pill of the cycle, you will glance up into the mirror and notice what people at work have been stopping to comment on: how good you're looking lately. You can see it yourself. That fuel pumping through the body, firing up the colour in your face. It's lust that'll do that to you, every time. Being the object of desire. Three weeks into it, and just look at the difference.

Once upon a time you would have said, confidently: show me someone who says they've never had a fantasy of being the Older Woman, and I'll show you a liar. It's like one of those dreams where you're walking through your ordinary familiar house feeling its confines and thinking nothing's going to change now, might as well accept it, when you notice a door you've never seen before. And you open it and on the other side is another whole possible living space, another alternative route through each day.

Before you get up, now, you think about what you're going to wear. You find lipstick, and put it on. You keep eye contact for longer than you need to.

Here's a dead giveaway: in the supermarket, in that third week, your hand will reach out and take a box of hair colour and it's the easiest thing in the world to appear the next day with red highlights. Who can blame you? This will induce recklessness: a 26-year-old guy ringing you up every night and saying he misses you when you're not together. Telling you you're beautiful and you shiver, feeling his hand move under your linen shirt (ironing clothes again!) and across your stomach. Sure, a little more effort's needed at thirty-nine. Of course you want that stomach to be as concave as it had been on the beach at twenty-two, back when you were busy prematurely ageing your skin, carefree and oblivious and immortal. You have to suck in your breath, under that hand. You have to stay on your guard.

You tell your friends where you met, at a film screening. You can't wait to talk about him.

It had been an industry preview with complimentary tickets, you say, and people seem to chat more when nobody's paid for their tickets. 'He asked me if his backpack bag thing was annoying me next to my feet, and I said no.'

'They're not called backpacks now,' Sandy interrupts. 'They're called *crumplers*.'

'Well, whatever. When the film ended he was taking a few notes and I asked him about it, we got chatting and went out for a drink.'

'Out for a drink where?'

'Mario's. And just talked for an hour about the film.'

'Aha,' said Helen. 'Mario's. Over-thirties lighting.' But you see she's listening as avidly as anyone, to learn how to chance it, getting something started gracefully.

For a while now, you've avoided looking at yourself in the full-length mirror in the bathroom by neglecting to put the ventilation fan on. You hurry to dry yourself and get out of there before the mirror unsteams. Life, if we hold it up to the light, contains many of these foolish rituals. Like the one you notice lately where you always turn off the bedside lamp before you slide into bed with him, and the way you don't wear your glasses at the movies.

You want his appreciation newly minted, you want to believe he actually can hardly believe his luck. The endorphins must bathe your brain with these possibilities. With every phone call, every new plan he proposes for the two of you, you start to believe you could maybe leave the bathroom fan on sometime soon, and deal with that scrutiny. You start thinking you actually have those rich chestnut highlights in your hair naturally. Well. You know the rest. You know how it all goes.

Then, a week into the contraceptives, you're ravenous. Standing there in the kitchen eating spoonfuls of rice out of the saucepan, chewing and staring at the notices under the fridge magnets. Walking through the house gnawing on chicken legs, buying croissants at morning tea. Back at home you take the packet of contraceptives out of the bathroom cupboard and read the side-effects again—*increased appetite, tendency to hirsuteness, loss of libido, double vision, nausea*—and resolve to eat less, use sunscreen more, avoid alcohol except in moderation. This demands vigilance. Six weeks now, and soon you will be going down the coast for the weekend, like a proper couple on a romantic getaway, and all you can think about is how your thighs will look in a swimsuit.

Six weeks, and in two more months you will be forty, and the friends are making jokes about a party to run this new guy through his paces—this thinking woman's toy boy, as they call him—an event it is impossible to comfortably imagine. Forty, and Sandy knows what a crumpler is because she has a thirteen-year-old son, whereas you, you have to keep smothering a rising panic that you've missed the bus. Thirteen years ago you were living in London, fervently avoiding any chance of children. Now you're one of those nuisance women obstetricians must hate, waking up to the alarm on your biological clock just before it runs itself down.

So you find yourself at the chemist buying the sunscreen for mature skin, the moisturiser with concealer that guarantees a visible difference. Forty, and your fertile years are waning away in a dwindling flush of denial and negation, each lost month rushing closer like concrete pylons on the female superhighway, a marker of defeat, and if you were honest, you would admit that every pill sticks in your throat like a sugar-coated lie. Instead you swallow it with eyes closed, the better to avoid seeing details in that mirror. All those permutations, all those possible side-effects.

While you're at the chemist, you buy another box of hair dye promising those living colour highlights. Your hair needs a wash—you glance at it in one of the make-up mirrors. Dark roots are showing through, an abrupt line drawn against the scalp like a growth ring on a tree, exposing a weak moment where you succumbed to vanity. Since you dyed it the chemicals have lightened it; the auburn highlights have disappeared. It looks kind of yellowish. Brassy, your mother would call it. Time to go to a salon and have a cut and colour, she would say, with that complacent little sigh acknowledging the mysterious burden of female duty.

You should leave it there, to grow out. But there is grey amongst the dark hair, a nasty cigarette-ash colour you tell yourself you haven't noticed before. In the privacy of your own bathroom you shake together the contents of two ammonia-smelling bottles of chemicals and cover up those roots. Even as you sit waiting the allotted time, feeling vain and foolish but wanting lustrous highlighted hair for the weekend, you happen to glance in the afternoon light at your neck and see the downy hairs on your chin and throat are silhouetted, and they are dark.

In strong light you can see them perfectly clearly. Another side-effect, just as the contraceptive packet predicted. So, naturally, you grab the tweezers and pull them out. But when you tilt your head into that hard light you see dark hairs coming through on your upper lip, too. Jesus, no. If you start yanking these you'll never be able to stop, you'll be like one of those bristly old women with moustaches, stiff hairs you can feel when you kiss.

So. More vigilance, you think, grimacing. Pluck and cover. Smirking into the mirror, then deciding it's one joke you'll never be able to tell him.

It's a slippery slope, once you start on it, once you've ignored that knock in the engine for long enough and it starts to miss occasionally as you career down some hill dazedly gripping the wheel.

At the beach the sun comes out and the sea glitters to the horizon, and Paul is content to sit and watch the surfers for a while. When you're twenty-six, obviously that's what you do, because it's still within the radar range of things you might conceivably try yourself. Then he goes and buys fish and chips and you eat them at a picnic table, everything dazzling and warm. But once that poison has started, once you're committed to giving yourself a measured dose of it every day, nothing's going to be enough. You have traded in your unselfconsciousness for this double-visioned state of standing outside yourself, watchful and tensed for exposure. You will despise yourself for every mouthful and for your insatiable hunger, and you will despise yourself more for breaking away from him as you walk out of the surf to hurry back to your towel to get your sarong and cover up. So that even as he grins at you sitting on the sand and says, 'Isn't this great?', a small, snarling bitter voice will be sounding in the back of your head saying: *Yeah. I'm sitting squinting into the sun getting crow's-feet and eating saturated fats. Great.*

Waiting for him to unlock the car to leave, don't, whatever you do, look at your silhouette in the reflection of the car window. It will show you nothing but hard contrast. In the solarised shadow and light, you will see lines on your forehead, and those ones etched between your nose and mouth, the awful twist of discontent. Old harridan lines.

Just get in the car. Put your sunglasses on, and get in the car.

And later, when he's not watching, feel disgusted scorn for yourself as you try to covertly open your bag and get out the factor-fifteen moisturiser, and put it on. Neck as well as face. Think of all the mornings when you get up and your neck and chest are creased like an old sheet. Jowls. Crepey skin. Turkey neck. Spinster aunt skin. Wonder if he wakes before you, and looks at those creases as you're asleep, exposed, in the bright morning light.

The ever-relentless sun, inescapable, beats down on you through the windscreen.

All those hours you mindlessly lay on your towel in your twenties, and tilted your face up into it, heedless. You look across at his face, and of course he doesn't care, he doesn't need to. He's got years.

Inexorable, this spiral down. Tell him later that no, really, you want the light off. Don't say a word about turning forty. When he says he loves you, some reflex from those side-effects will mean you won't let yourself believe it. Censor everything. Swallow the pill. Remember this: let the smallest reference to babies slip, and you can kiss this guy goodbye.

Funny how the dye seems to have missed the odd grey hair, which seem stronger and wirier than the others. And the way you only notice them when you can't really lean forward and do anything about them—when you're looking in the mirror of a change room, for example, in a fairly expensive department store on your afternoon off, and the sight of your own cellulite (all those chips!) so disgusts you and saps your energy that you doubt whether you can actually get dressed again and drag yourself out of there, away from that ridiculous lingerie or the jeans you've chosen. Why are you even wasting your time with this guy? Why don't you find someone your own age who might actually be interested in a late bid for last-minute parenthood, someone who might be in for the long haul? You're too pathetic to believe yourself. And just as you grab your hairbrush after changing back into your stupid frump clothes, just as you think for a minute you'll at least brush your hair, you notice in these unforgiving overhead lights those dark roots coming through again already—any fool could see your colour's not natural. Your hair sits lank and dried-out against your head.

You've got to stop this. But you can't help yourself. While you're in the hair salon buying shampoo for colour-treated hair, you find yourself making an appointment for a leg wax. You will be hairless. Forty is the new thirty. You will be smooth, controlled, gym-toned, with the body of a woman in her late twenties, lushly in her prime and way ahead of the game.

And the voice you hear now as you sit in the salon leafing through the magazines before your appointment will be a whiny, accusing one, nitpicking and obsessive, poking you on the shoulder saying: *Look, Goldie Hawn, nearly sixty. Look, Sharon Stone, slim and elegant, had a baby at forty-four.*

The receptionist says, 'This your first visit?' Her fingernails are curved like talons, alternately purple and yellow, and you see they are fake and stuck on with superglue. They are so long she can hardly write — but she can hardly write anyway, breathing laboriously as she prints your details in big Grade Five letters. Then into the back room and up onto the crackling paper sheet. Butcher's paper for a slab of meat. You make nervous small talk.

'Do you wax guys?' you blurt.

'All the time.' The girl stirs wax implacably, arranges things on the counter like a dental nurse. 'You'd be surprised.' You lie back. She chats on.

'Guys come in here, want their backs waxed, their arses.'

'You're kidding.'

'Nope. I do everything. You wouldn't believe it. A week before Mardi Gras, or when there's a bike race or the City to Surf, I'm booked out.'

Suddenly there is a hot stroke of wax on your shin, a pause, then blinding pain.

'*Ow.* Jesus.'

'Haven't had them done for a while, that's why it hurts more.'

'Actually this is my first time ever.'

'Really? Oh well, it won't take long.'

Another rip that brings tears to your eyes.

'Brazilians are all the go now,' she says. 'You want pain, boy …'

'Don't tell me.'

She tilts your leg, ices on some more wax, rips it away.

'Yep, everything. Completely hairless. Like a Barbie doll.'

You shudder and lie back, willing it to be over. Like having a cavity drilled, you try to take your thoughts away. Paul, and what he would say if he could see you now. Think then about your first argument, the other night. 'Don't tell me what I'm going to do next,' he'd finally fumed. 'And Jesus, will you just relax and stop worrying about your weight? How much reassurance do you need?'

'I don't need reassurance.'

'Yes, you do. It's so bloody tiring. It's like you've already decided to end it and you're just waiting for me to slip up so you can blame me.'

You'd opened and closed your mouth like a stunned fish. A wave of nausea. You'd clenched your jaw, saying nothing. *Don't cry*, you'd ordered yourself, *don't you dare. Mascara running. Haggard. Lines. Ugly. Old.*

'Let's just light a candle then, if you don't want the lamp on,' he'd said later in bed, at his place. And you'd shaken your head, taken the matches from him.

'No,' you'd answered. 'Let's not. Really. I like the dark.'

She's up to your groin and you feel the wax getting daubed around your undies line. She holds the skin taut and pulls. It's excruciating.

'Bloody hell!' you gasp.

'Yeah, the pubic hairs always hurt more — deeper roots.'

'And people have the whole lot ripped out?'

'All the time.'

You look down at the reddened patch and see tiny prick marks of blood appearing where the hairs have been yanked out. It feels like you've had a layer of skin torn off. Like you've been peeled.

'God, how could they stand it?'

She considers, moving her chewing gum around her mouth. 'They reckon it looks clean.'

'Clean?'

'Sexy. Their boyfriends ask 'em to do it, they say.'

Rip. She's on the other ankle. *Clean*, you think. Prepubescent, more like it. Like pink latex, like a blow-up fantasy doll, that sickly plastic smell of Barbie. The rip across the knee works like a quick, stinging, sobering slap to the face, finally waking you up.

'That'll do,' you hear yourself say.

'But we're only halfway through.' She stops, staring, rotating a glob of slipping yellow wax slowly on the hovering spatula.

'That's okay, I'll pay for the whole thing. I just ... that's it.'

'It's not hurting that much, is it?'

You swing your tingling legs off the table and reach for your jeans.

She's looking at you, moving the chewy around in her lip-glossed mouth.

'Okay, then,' she says with a shrug. And, half-finished, like someone released from custody, you're out of there.

Later that night, there'll be tiny dark patches on your bare legs when you take your jeans off, where wax has stuck spots of lint to the skin, but you will pull a sheet over your legs instead of jumping up instantly and washing it off in the shower. Your energy for subterfuge seems spent now; like the tank's empty. In the dark, all other senses are more acute; the brush of skin on skin, the scent of hair, a whisper blooming next to you on the pillow; risky secrets that cannot be taken back. You will feel things coast to a stop, sharpened into wakefulness, and steady yourself. You open your mouth and set whatever's coming next in motion.

'I'll be forty in a fortnight,' you say.

Impossible to gauge his real, unadorned reaction to that news. You'll have to turn the light on for that.

Angel

'You don't say much, do ya?' said the lady in the shop on the ground floor of the flats when I first came here. I shook my head and smiled. The tone in her voice was one I had grown to recognise. In Vietnamese, a slight inflection can change the meaning of a word entirely, in English this can apply to a whole phrase. As she scooped up my change her voice maintained that it was just being friendly, but there was an inflection in there meant only for me. In Australia many people take silence for rudeness, for not enough gratitude. If I were really grateful for being here, I would talk endlessly. Thank you, thank you, thank you for having me. That is what the feeling is, in the flats and in English class: an expressionless resentment at my failure to play my part.

'Talk about your new country,' my tutor would say, reading that suggestion out of a book on how to teach people like us.

'I like the trees,' the students would say, flat and careful. 'I like the sea.'

I don't like the sea, I would think to myself. I spent two months on the sea, waiting for my turn to sip the water, knowing as people vomited that they would be the ones to die.

'Let's hear from Mai,' the tutor would say, and everyone would turn, ready to watch my difficulties. Wanting to get the language themselves, this barely comprehensible thing that would allow them their driving licences and jobs in the T-shirt factory in Smith Street or Champion Dimsims in Ascot Vale.

'I like the sea, too,' I would say, the obedient student. My father used to say I was the best student at the school in my town, the family scholar. I learned by keeping quiet, but this is not the way you learned in Australia. When I passed very well in my English class, my tutor looked at me with the same expression as the lady in the shop.

'You don't say much, but you take it all in, don't you?' she said, an accusing finger on my diploma. Why is silence so worthy of suspicion? You can choose to talk or choose to not talk. But take it all in: yes, that part is true. I take everything in, and in bed at night I lie rocking on a tide of it, whole scenes and conversations, faces I will not forget, even if I wanted to. After the boat, there was a child I went on caring for at the camp who didn't speak for a whole five months. I worried that the authorities would think she was a slow learner. That was not the problem. The problem was she was a fast learner; she took it all in. When we got into the harbour we were news, not because of our plight so much as something unusual that had occurred on our boat.

'They want to ask you about the shark attack,' said the interpreter, nervous, and the people with the camera equipment had made a movement, a hopeful, craning movement, towards this child. Whether she spoke or not, I could tell she would be the one they made the story about.

She hadn't spoken since this thing happened, and she didn't speak now. She didn't say a word till three months later, when other authorities came to the camp and news spread around, a whispered, desperate rumour, that they were going to give preference to all the children under six. This child, who was eight, was with me and she suddenly wrenched away and rushed to the table where the men were sitting with their papers and slapped her hand down. She spoke to them in perfect English, the first two words she'd uttered for five months.

'I'm five,' she said.

I, too, broke my silence that day with a lie.

'I am her mother,' I said.

She is a chatterbox now, my daughter. My father, if he were alive, would be proudly calling her the family scholar now. But at night-time when I go into her room, I find myself looking at her small head and thinking: *Inside there is the boat and the shark and the slipping over the side of bodies, the watching for pirates and chewing on bleeding teeth.* And I think: *That is enough to take in.*

Scenes, conversations, faces. Sometimes just a picture—the stillness of my father's shoulders as he got up from the table to be taken away, waiting while they turned over everything in the house. I went to speak and he shook his head just once at me. His hands waiting, still, on the table. A chicken came in watchfully in the quiet and pecked very carefully at some grain the soldiers had tipped out.

I saw one of those soldiers again, only two or three months ago. I was at the Footscray market and I saw him crossing the street in a big crowd of people. He looked just the same except he had a leather jacket on now.

'There is so much evil in the world.' That is what the lady downstairs says. I go to a different market now, with her and some other ladies on the Community Centre bus. She invites me down to her flat to drink coffee and talks very fast about her relatives in her country, too fast for me. She gets out photograph albums, shows me pictures, gets her two noisy daughters to dress up in their national clothes to show me. 'English,' says Gabriella, 'who can understand it? In Spanish, the language has rules, and they are sensible, every tense matches every verb, every letter is pronounced correctly. The war,' she tells me, 'has given Central American Spanish a new verb: to disappear.'

'I am sorry,' I say. 'I am confused.'

Gabriella explains. 'To disappear somebody,' she says. 'An active verb. People there are *disappeared*. Do you understand?'

Then she plays a video. The pictures are blurry; there are people running along the street, police, pictures of bodies and women crying outside the hospital, holding up photos. More pictures of bodies and soldiers training. Gabriella watches and cries, passes me a photo over the coffee cups of a sister at her fifteenth birthday. 'Not even political,' says Gabriella, rocking back and forth on her little boat of grief, 'a student, nothing more.' I have no more room to take anything else in. I have no national dresses, no photos to show in return. There is no point in saying anything.

From my window I cannot watch my daughter playing in the playground. My flat faces the wrong direction, towards the new freeway. She tells me I worry too much, that she does not like her friends to see me sitting on the bench down there keeping my eye on them all. That is what she says: keeping my eye on them. It is a strange expression; it makes me think of an angel. I have a blind over the window now. One day I was looking out, not expecting anything and not really seeing, when something went past—a flutter of clothing, fast as blinking. I did not go downstairs.

Gabriella came up. She expected that I would know the girl because she was Vietnamese, and said that she had jumped with an empty purse in her hand. She paused after she told me this, expecting me to say something. I shook my head, looking at Gabriella's own hands, clutching tissues and her own throat, wringing themselves with all the evil in the world.

There is no angel there to keep an eye on my daughter. Vietnamese children are often approached because it is their reflex to be polite to adults. Sometimes I catch a glimpse of her from the balcony outside the lifts, and see her small shining head with all that it contains going back and forth on the swing and the monkey bars. One day last week she stopped playing there. She stayed in the flat, colouring in her schoolwork, not talking. A silence rose between us, waiting for me to form the question, and in that silence I heard the shuffle of a soldier's boot, the quick hard tap as the chicken struck in the stillness.

'Why aren't you at the adventure playground?' I asked.

Her hand coloured and coloured with her new textas. It was the sea around Australia, light blue for shallow water, dark blue for deep. The paper was softly tearing. I put my hand over her hand, the hand that had slapped the table, so strong was its owner's will. Now it stopped colouring, and was still.

'A man came,' she said.

There have been five days between her telling me this and now, this moment. She stopped talking then, but she showed me what he had done and led me down to the little storeroom for bins behind the laundry. Showed me with a tiny gesture who it was, as we crossed the road to the school. Two friends walked ahead with their mothers and she looked at me and pointed again.

'Mai knows more than she says; she takes it all in.' That is what Gabriella and the others are saying about me. They think I know more about the body than I let on, because I still don't say anything. Silence instils suspicion, so they are anxious to talk to the police, smothering their fear of uniforms and trying to hear the layers between what is said and what is not said. They tell the police everything they can think of, and the second time the police come to see me they joke that my neighbours all think I am the mystery woman. I am not a mystery, I want to say to them, I am my daughter's angel. They try very hard to make me talk; they say they need a statement. The lady in the shop, they say, believes it was me she saw and is making a statement. They now wish to search through the flat. Their voices are as careful as the students' in English class, slow and deliberate, stumbling over long difficult words and without inflection. In the silence before I speak there is the creak of a boot, hands lying flat on the table.

'There is so much evil in the world,' I say. How different this is to the other day, when my father stood his last minutes in the kitchen, collecting himself. There everybody knew a disappearance was to occur, no statement was required. Here everyone seems to talk at once, to all try repeating the questions using different words, as if language, not silence, is the code. A bag of clothes is overturned in the bedroom. I hear the plastic bag being shaken, and think of that soldier's face as he waited for my father to rise, as empty as when he stepped across the pedestrian crossing in Barkly Street holding his mobile phone. Now they are whispering to each other in the kitchen and talking loudly into my face, telling me they have found the knife.

Now they are telling me I have the right to remain silent.

Seizure

If it hadn't been Helen's turn to collect the coffees she wouldn't have seen it. She was carrying the tray back to work when a man in front of her—an ordinary-looking man in a grey suit, a little overweight, hurrying—suddenly sprawled to the ground. His keys and briefcase and a mobile phone went skidding from his outstretched hand and across the concrete.

About ten people stopped. Helen, heart thudding with uselessness, put the tray of coffees on the ground and picked up the man's belongings, thinking, *he's not getting up*, and feeling the day lurch out of ordinariness. She stood up self-consciously, wondering if her hesitation was losing him vital moments and the oxygen was ebbing from his brain because she didn't know how to do CPR. When she turned back, though, another man had detached himself from the milling crowd and was turning the injured man's grazed head to the side, loosening his collar. He glanced up at Helen.

'He's fitting,' he said. 'Epilepsy.' Then he turned back to the unconscious man on the pavement. 'You're okay. Take it easy now.'

She watched the way he took a pen from a pocket and worked it carefully and patiently between the prone man's teeth. One of the passers-by had something to say to their companion about that, as if they were watching a documentary.

'So he doesn't swallow his tongue,' they said. 'Choke on it.'

'Epileptic fit,' Helen heard muttered from the onlookers. She crouched and tucked the keys and mobile phone back into the unconscious man's suit pocket, stood his briefcase next to him. She studied his face, red and sweaty with a swelling lump where he'd smacked the pavement, resting close to the other man's knees. She imagined him five minutes before, finishing a cigarette and talking on his mobile, alert and purposeful, striding back to work with dignity intact. Now this.

'You're all right,' said the crouching man soothingly, and Helen watched, surrendering any responsibility with relief, as he reached over and smoothed the man's hair out of his eyes. Suddenly the unconscious man's mouth laboured and he vomited. The onlookers moved on at that, with distaste. But Helen was still drawn to those hands, lifting his head, shifting the pen, grabbing a handkerchief and wiping, never hesitating.

'You're right. Everything's okay.'

Helen felt her face flush with someone else's humiliation, and something else. That another stranger, passing randomly

DARK ROOTS

on the street, could be the agent of such unconditional compassion. She tore her eyes away from those ministering hands, and said: 'Is he going to be OK, or shall I call an ambulance?'

'I think we'll be right—I'll take care of it. It's just a kind of seizure. He'll be fine in a few minutes.' He glanced up at her as he spoke, smiled and added, 'Thanks for stopping, though.'

He was not a man who commanded attention. Later Helen could hardly remember what his face looked like; mild, freckled, unremarkable—like someone who fixed your phone, someone who sold you a stereo unit or whitegoods, some blurry identikit picture with features you wouldn't look at twice. All she saw was his sandy hair, his thin narrow shoulders in an old checked shirt and the pink sunburnt line across his nose. He knelt there patiently, one knee in pooling vomit, not moving, and she thought that if she was lying in the road after an accident, he'd be the person she'd want to stay with her. The unconscious man's hand twitched, opened and closed. His head would be splitting when he woke up, thought Helen.

She picked up the tray of coffees and experienced the strange sensation of not wanting to leave. She pictured herself back at the office, relating what had happened, and could envision the same milling interest of the crowd that had stopped, expressions of disgust when she mentioned vomiting, the women grimacing with polite sympathy and Alan, the office know-all, regaling them all with details of epilepsy.

She wanted to stay here, of all places, and … what? Just rest. Witness more of that kindness. She made herself walk away, but her feet dragged, as if something lay there she had neglected to notice. She felt thrown by a sudden, dull fatigue. As she walked, she tore her own coffee out of the tray and had a mouthful. It had upset her, that was all — that poor man, confident and unsuspecting and suddenly felled. She turned back and saw the sandy-haired guy take the unconscious man's briefcase and with all the tenderness in the world slide it gently under his head, and go on waiting. Her heart ached. She wouldn't say a word to anyone at the office.

Helen had lived with Steve for seven years. When her friends talked about their relationships to Helen it often seemed they were avidly describing characters in a TV show or movie, each with their own motivations and reasons, their flaws and failings. The conversations and arguments they related seemed pointed and polished, like scripts.

When her girlfriends talked about Steve they said he was *dynamic* and *charismatic*, and Helen would find herself filing away those character traits, trying to step back to get an overview of the plot. The way she related the storyline, Steve was the perennial enthusiast and she was the reluctant one, lagging behind.

'It's never dull,' she would concede with a smile, feeling how Steve's plans pulled her along like an undertow. This weekend, for example, he'd talked her into going bushwalking again and when she got home that night he had a map spread out. *Ah, yes—the gorge*, she thought as she put her keys on the kitchen bench.

'Hi,' said Steve, absorbed in mapping. 'Good day?'

'Um … yeah.'

She watched him lean over the table with a highlighter pen hovering.

'Do you want to get some Thai takeaway?' she said.

'No, no, I'm making puttanesca. Just give me a sec with this and I'll get started.'

He came over and gave her an absent-minded kiss. Steve was big and broad-shouldered and for a second she was enveloped in one of his distracted one-armed hugs, the elbow clamped briefly around her neck, before he moved back to the table.

'Okay. But can you please make it not too hot?'

'Sure. Just mild,' he said, his eyes back on the map. 'Just a mere shaving of hot salami.'

She could have written that part of the script in her sleep. She was about to nag, to tell him that he always said that and it was always too hot, but stopped herself. She waited for him to look up at her again, leaning against the bench there in silence. What she wanted, now she thought about it, was for him to look more carefully at her and ask her if anything was wrong, sense her mood from across the room and tune into it, maybe even ask her if she still felt like doing an eight-kilometre hike the next day. But he was focused on his pen, curving neatly down the page in luminous yellow, and then refolding the map carefully leaving the relevant sections open. She could wait all she wanted; he wasn't going to look up.

In their bedroom, both their daypacks rested on top of the week's washing she'd folded that morning. Helen unzipped hers and smelt the familiar, unwelcome odour of apples and sunscreen, took out some brochure she'd picked up from somewhere about a winery and tossed it in the bin. Outside, the TV and the news waited, and her special glass in the cupboard for her first red out of the cask, but instead of going back out there she sat on the bed and paged through a *Country Life* magazine for a long time. When she finished she felt listless and sated, slightly nauseated by the perfumy smell of the gloss pages. Steve was right, they were a stupid thing to buy; he stacked them up beside the toilet for a joke when they had guests. Helen leaned back on the pillow and lay there pondering, feeling something—energy, probably—slackly spooling out of her, like fishing line following a lead sinker from an open reel. The pillowcase itched. Her waistband felt too tight. She anticipated the following day like a visit to the dentist. She recognised that familiar, unwilling lassitude, and summoned what she needed to fight it off.

It was Friday night. She would rouse herself and put away their washing. Steve, busy with his planning, would finally serve up dinner at about 9.30. The puttanesca would just about take the roof of her mouth off. He would apologise mildly between mouthfuls and say he couldn't understand it, he'd put hardly any chilli in at all. She would say it didn't matter and make some toasted sandwiches, stack the dishwasher, marvelling that he'd managed to use every pot and saucepan they owned. Friday night, everything about normal.

'I saw someone have an epileptic seizure today,' she said later in bed.

'Yeah? What happened?'

'He just fell over onto the concrete while I was out at lunchtime. Someone helped him.'

There was a silence, then Steve said, 'Funny how they're called *petit mal* and *grand mal*, isn't it? Epileptic fits.'

He still surprised her, after seven years, with the nuggets of knowledge he stored somewhere in his head. When they played trivia games with friends, he seemed to know odd, esoteric things that suggested another whole personality, one she had never met.

'I've never heard that,' she answered.

'Yeah, it means little bad and big bad. The *grand mal* being the one where you black out and collapse and so on. They reckon sometimes the people wake up and can't remember a thing about it, like the brain just runs a bit of blank tape.'

'Well, it was a big bad,' she said. 'This other guy knelt down and just looked after him. I found myself standing there just watching him.' She hesitated. 'I mean, I felt completely helpless, but kind of … mesmerised. Drawn to it.'

She felt herself pausing again, waiting for him to ask her what had happened next.

He yawned. 'Really? Maybe you should enrol in a first-aid course,' he replied.

Steve, she reflected to herself, would have dealt with it better than her, would have had a cool head in a crisis. He was good at solutions. *Do a course if you're bored. Go for a walk if you feel so restless.* Everything seemed logical to him, a simple matter of rational cause and effect. *You wouldn't wake up feeling sick if you didn't drink red wine before you go to bed,* he'd remind her when she complained; and then, *Well, you told me to tell you next time you did it.*

Helen let the subject rest. She didn't want them to stay awake. Something was going wrong with their sex life where everything would seem fine between them until the very moment when she felt his questioning hand reach over, and she would remember again a squeamish unwillingness she'd put out of her mind until then. She hated the silence that sprang up between them as his palm would drop heavily onto her hip, the way he always seemed to forget where she liked to be touched. She would feel breathless; not with desire, she recognised with alarm, but with a kind of buried discomfort. Discussing it was something her girlfriends would describe as a no-go zone; but this unspoken space had grown and flourished into a volume of silence between them, something pitted with snags there in the dark, so that every manoeuvre between them in bed was now stiff with things unsaid.

She listened for the telltale lengthening of his breathing, which would mean it wouldn't be broached, and for the wash of relief under the uneasy sense that this avoidance was being made worse and worse by ignoring it. Helen's girlfriends, in their heart-to-hearts, all seemed to find their men lacking in a certain physical demonstrativeness, and Helen felt the same, although Steve would point out that he had noticed this in men himself and was consciously trying to rectify it. It was true, he made efforts to be physically affectionate outside bed, but if she had to find a word to describe his attentions she would have said 'brotherly'. He would kiss her, like he did anyone else, briefly on the cheek. He put his hands in his pockets when they were out together so they didn't look like some cliché of coupledom. After such casual, careless gestures of affection she knew she should muster something else for what passed between them in private, when she felt that hand on her skin in the darkness. Instead there was this sense of obligation growing steadily into a faint hum of resentment at the idea that all that fraternal arm-squeezing should have been enough to keep her responsive.

Man-handled, she thought now as she lay there, and checked herself with surprise: *Listen to me.* She stared into the dark, her mind roaming.

That sunburnt line across that guy's nose, she thought sleepily. Probably played sport. Saturday with his mates playing cricket, maybe. Mates he still had from school. The easy intuitions of long friendships.

When she finally fell asleep, she dreamed she and Steve were on daytime television, being interviewed about keeping relationships harmonious. Steve was showing the admiring studio audience a housework roster he had devised outlining equitable task-sharing based on mutual understanding and respect, a gesture that brought envious sighs and ripples of applause from the female viewers. The second page of the roster outlined agreed-upon daily gestures and displays of love. He glanced across at Helen, smiling, and she smiled back, nodding as he talked about compromise and inviting cameras into their home any time to see how it worked. Their friends were in the audience, ready to step up to the microphone to testify and bear witness.

'You're one lucky woman,' said Oprah to Helen as the alarm went off. Steve jumped out of bed, raking the curtains back to let in the sunrise, and rummaged in his chest of drawers.

'I forgot to pack tweezers,' he said, 'in case you get a tick again.'

He smiled at her radiantly, good-looking even at 6.30 in the morning. He glanced out at the clear morning with a conductor's sweeping gesture of pleasure at the day, pleasure she knew she was meant to share, but it looked through her squinting eyes somehow proprietorial, as if even the clouds cleared and the sun rose obediently at his command.

In the car, she drove while he read interesting bits out of the paper to her. Turning onto the freeway, she tried to be philosophical about the prospect ahead of her. She was being stupid. She'd agreed to go on the bushwalk, and Steve loved it when they got out of the city, and she knew she was lucky to live somewhere where you could get to such a beautiful place so easily, she knew all that. It was one of their shared interests, Steve told other people, and she wasn't going to whinge about it. Tomorrow they could go out to a café for brunch, sit in calm virtuous silence and read the papers and eat croissants. If she just went and walked through the bush with him today, she could have a day off. That would be the deal.

He didn't make her camp so much any more, thank God. Although now, sitting with the road directory on his lap, he was trying to convince her that both of them should go on the Great Australian Bike Ride together this year. She drove, trying hard to muster enthusiasm.

'You'd love it,' Steve was saying, and she felt the same prickle of irritation she'd felt as a teenager when her old sports teacher had kept telling her how much better she'd feel after a run round the oval. Both of them so certain they knew what she needed, both exerting a confident authority that expected to prevail in the end. She would be compliant, she knew, swept along in a kind of slipstream of Steve's gusto for everything. Last year she'd begged off the bike ride, saying she felt stiff and unfit after a bout of flu. He had gone anyway, with some other friends.

If Steve really did make a roster like in her dream, Helen thought now, you could bet it wouldn't be fastened to the fridge with a frivolous heart-shaped magnet, or even the phone number for the local pizza shop. It would have to be a magnet the council gave you when you paid your rates, informing you what nights your paper and bottles would be picked up for recycling. It would serve a purpose.

'Is there a film festival or something on this weekend?' she said to Steve. 'Or were we meant to go to someone's place for lunch?'

'Nope,' he answered, sprawled in the passenger seat in

his monster hiking boots. She could smell the waterproofing gel he'd put on them the night before.

'I can't help thinking I'm going to realise what it is later, and kick myself.'

'There's nothing. The weekend's all ours to do exactly what we want with it.'

'Hey, read me my stars,' she said, watching for the turn-off.

'The horoscope? Don't be ridiculous,' he said, and she noticed with another little spurt of frustration that he'd thrown the magazine and the review section she liked into the back. 'Listen, here's something on that Dutch election.'

Her head cleared as he read. Impossible to complain — the things that annoyed her about Steve were such petty, trivial things. Not even worth putting into words. She imagined how whiny she'd sound: *You never let me read the television section, even though I've bought the paper. You never tell me I look nice when we go out somewhere. You never want to hold my hand when we're walking along.* Ludicrous. Just small prickles of anger like those sudden headaches that faded away just as fast, accumulating and dissipating like clouds in the face of a beaming, good-natured sun.

Little bads, she thought as she submitted to politics in the Netherlands.

As they parked the car and got ready, she caught sight of some other people in the park lying under a tree on a blanket, lazing in the shade with their books. Lucky bastards. It would be pointless to even voice her black mood; Steve would only ignore it and patiently, even-temperedly, wait for her to snap out of it.

'This is going to be great,' he said now, still oblivious, as he waited for her to collect her things and lock the car. 'Hey, Helen, look; you'll have to repack that.' He gestured to her backpack, lumpy with raincoat and lunch, and laughed. 'Give it to me, I'll re-do it. It's bound to annoy you after a while if you walk with it like that.'

She slung it off stonily and handed it to him, watching his hands open the zips and rearrange her things inside, patting them down and folding them more exactly.

All she could think of were those other hands, soothing someone back to consciousness. The ordinary kindness of a calm gesture. Like he was a ministering angel, she thought now.

They walked to the Parks and Wildlife shelter; an arrangement of laminated posters of native animals they would possibly sight on their walk and a topography map of the park mounted between green poles under a corrugated iron roof. Helen gravitated into that slice of shade, dawdling and reading the history of the park as Steve skimmed it, keen to hit the track.

She rested her hands on the long perspex-sealed display case as Steve rapped on it with a finger.

'Lucky we've brought our own map,' he said. 'Look at that.'

Helen looked down vaguely. She was aware again of something long and taut being pulled from her—a line, a wick, playing itself out silently, steady and unchecked. She felt it cease abruptly as it reached some finite point, caught on something silent and dark somewhere and held fast. Under her hands she saw that the perspex seal had failed and that seasons of moisture and glaring sun had faded the map, where the shade missed it, down to a few pale bleached lines stretching to the curling edges, the whole thing spotted with spores of black mould. She didn't want to move, didn't want to tear herself away.

She broke her gaze finally and looked up to see Steve ahead, on the path already, waiting for her. Soon he would turn around again and set off alone, thinking she'd catch up dutifully in a few minutes. She saw herself for a few seconds through his eyes: *Being strange today, best to ignore it, she'll come around.*

There was a word, meanwhile, which stayed tugging faintly and insistently on the end of that line, just outside her consciousness; if she stayed quiet and didn't break the spell, the word would come to her. She felt sleepy and disoriented, but the word would come to her, and then she would know what was missing. She went on staring down at the blurred, ruined map in a trance of waiting. This is how it would feel, she thought, to wake up with that blank, jarred feeling, sprawled out, exposed on the pavement in public, nothing solved, no explanation, a *grand mal*. But stroked awake, cared for, so you'd know you wouldn't have to fend for yourself. Those hands like wings.

Cherish, Helen thought finally, feeling the cool relief of locating it settle over her as she slid off her pack and turned back to the shade of the trees. *Cherish*. That was the word.

The Light of Coincidence

I am not one of life's success stories. I'm first on the list when they're laying people off. I'm pulled over for speeding the day my car runs out of rego. My fly gapes open at parties. But one thing's for certain: I have a gift. I attract coincidence the way some people attract lightning. I could be browsing at a second-hand bookstall and pull out a book I remember from my high school English days and open it up and find my own name inside. This kind of thing has happened more times than I care to remember. Once when I used to have my own stall at Camberwell I was sitting leafing through the biography of Carl Jung, just at the chapter where he's talking about how the gods come into our lives to test our characters but they come disguised, so we miss them. I'm thinking about this, about keeping the book and reading on, when a punter who'd been poking round for a while clears his throat.

'Hi there,' I say, keeping my finger on the page and

having a sip of my coffee.

'Hi,' he says. 'Nice collection.'

'Thanks. After anything in particular?'

'Well,' he says, consulting a bit of paper out of his wallet, 'I'm hunting for a paperback biography of Carl Jung.'

That's the kind of thing I mean. Once I got to the market early and bought something unusual — a green suede jacket. Not a common item. But I was there and just cruising around the stalls and bought it and put it on and, of course, it was a perfect fit. I walked off feeling pretty chuffed with myself — I'd been looking for something like it for nigh on eight months — when I go down the next row and what do I see but another green suede jacket. Cheaper than the one I'd bought. See what I mean? It's like there's a lesson, there's the signal, but I can't quite get what the point is.

So when I needed $700 in a hurry, I kind of back-pedalled and had a think about picking up on those disguised gods. Those windows of opportunity. Had my bargain antennae tuned and ready to go.

You've got to get early to Camberwell. Round dawn you can spot the dealers with eyes like minesweepers. I hate the place at 6.00 a.m., like it again by 8.00, and by 11.00, when the sun's beating down and folks are walking round with armfuls of flowers and a felafel, it's the king of markets to me. The world is there spread out on a blanket, in all its shabbiness and failure and optimism and triumph.

Seven hundred dollars, I was thinking to myself as I strolled, eyes peeled for something antique, something overlooked, one of those stories you hear—brass lamps painted with old house paint, grandad's priceless stamp collection, the book with the spidery author's signature and faded annotations. Open your mind, I told myself, and invite those gods in. It had to be coincidence that I was humming a violin concerto when I spotted the violin. Snapped the locks and checked inside—nice colour, good wood. I knew bugger-all about violins, but I was in that kind of mood. Hairs on the back of the neck rising. Feeling lucky, feeling like I was due for a break. I held it up as if I knew a thing or two about violins and squinted along the neck, or whatever it's called. Ah yes. They've called in the violin expert, the top man. There's been no expense spared. The pegs looked all right, though. Could be ivory.

It was a long shot, a very long one, but like I said, I attract the kinds of things that people shake their heads over. I looked inside the violin—some handwritten name on the wood in there. My palms were sweaty. It felt good, it felt valuable, it felt like it might be worth something to my friend in the business.

'How much for the violin, then?'

And got the answer you crave.

'I'm not sure ... it's my brother's ... he's gone overseas to live and he doesn't play any more. We're cleaning out his wardrobe.'

Oh, thank you gods of coincidence and lessons whose significance is beyond me.

'So what's it worth to you?' I made my voice non-committal; I should have been in TV. I put it back in the case and made my eyes rove over other stuff on the table and, to aid my charade, actually picked up a 400-piece jigsaw puzzle in a box well secured with masking tape and looked at it seriously. A picture of the Vienna skyline. I gazed at it with a studied lack of interest.

'How about $100?' she said. Tentatively. Would it have been bad karma to haggle?

'Tell you what,' I said. 'Chuck in the jigsaw and I'll give you $80.'

She shrugged. Bonanza. Bullseye. Too bad, shifty dealers and hawk-eyed music buffs. This priceless instrument is mine. I gave her four twenties and beat a retreat. Past the guy who thinks he's Elvis, who was sounding more like Tom Waits by this stage of the morning. Past the kransky hot-dog stall and the litter of domestic cast-offs at the northern end of the market. Dropped fifty cents into a busker's case. And sloped off home. Where, just out of interest, I opened the jigsaw box.

Let me tell you a story, a connoisseur story of coincidence. There I was trundling down the 'down' escalator at Flinders Street Station, jammed into crowds of people, when who should I see but an old girlfriend I hadn't seen in ten years going up the escalator across the way. She was in blue. Oblivious to my calling and waving, she disappeared up the moving stairwell. I was seized with an overwhelming urge to say hello, and at the bottom I turned and raced back up her escalator and was deposited in the whirlpool of commuters on the ground floor. No sign of her. I raced outside and saw her blue jumper, sixty metres or so up Swanston Street, so I barrelled across the road and caught up. Tender greetings followed.

'What a coincidence,' I said. 'I just looked up at the right time to see you on the escalator in the station.' A puzzled frown crossed her face.

'I wasn't in the station,' she said.

They can pack a cruel stomach-punch, these kinds of coincidences. They can knock the breath out of you, make you look around for a camera, some cosmic punchline. As I picked off the masking tape around the jigsaw box, I was thinking of the violin and taking it to my man Lewis in Victoria Street for a valuation. But I should have known better, of course. Because what lay inside the box, nestled among the pieces, was a plastic bag of white powder. Don't get me wrong, I've never dabbled, but I'm not stupid. We were talking half a kilo of the hard stuff here.

I put the package down and thought for a while. Thought of the brother who'd gone overseas and left his well-meaning family to their spring-cleaning. Thought about needing seven hundred bucks and kissing goodbye my rent arrears and parking-infringement debts at the same time. Thought about the disguise a god might come in to test my character.

As I sat there I noticed two edge pieces of the jigsaw and pulled them out. Poked around and stuck a few bits of sky together. By the time I'd decided to go and see Lewis, I'd put together the whole top edge and half the skyline.

'Interested in an old and rare violin, miraculously unearthed at a local flea market?' I asked Lewis, swinging the case in front of him. He came around the counter, wiping his hands.

'Always interested. Hasn't happened yet, though, so don't hold your breath.'

'Lewis, I may have something here to restore your faith in miracles.'

He grinned, rubbed his eye. 'Put it out the back. I'll lock up and buy you a beer.'

Sitting in the pub the words jostled in my mouth, waiting to be aired: *Lewis, how hard would it be to offload half a kilo of heroin?* I drank a mouthful of beer, drowning them. Because I was scared of the answer, to tell you the truth. Scared of Lewis's barking, incredulous laugh and his words that would commit me to the next step. *Easy as this*, Lewis would say, drawing on his smoke, pointing. *See that guy sitting over there?* Then I would be lost.

'Give us a call about that fiddle,' I said, picking up my keys.

'No worries. But no promises.'

Back home, I filled in the rest of the skyline, a park and a cathedral. The bag of heroin lay there on the mantelpiece, looking for all the world like a wrapped-up bag of snags for a barbecue. What would old Carl Jung have suggested, I wonder. I didn't have the book, I'd sold it to that guy for three bucks, just to see the pleased light of coincidence dawning on his face.

I filled out the buildings on the jigsaw, sorted the pieces

into grass and brick, started working in from the bottom. Stone interlocked with stone, a blur of colour became a floral border in the park. I put on the cricket, and thought about friends who used, friends who were addicted, friends who'd gone into that one-way love affair and were no longer around.

If I hadn't been thinking about Jung, I wouldn't have done it. But I sat there piecing the jigsaw together and it came to me that old Carl actually came from Vienna, and here I was at 2.30 in the morning reconstructing it, and I had to give a smile for the hidden camera when I realised that just one piece was missing, and it was a doorway. I got up and tore a hole in the plastic bag and emptied the heroin down the toilet. I thought of lots of things as I flushed it; money problems mainly, but most of all how suddenly, bone-achingly tired I was. I went to bed and slept without dreaming, and didn't wake up until the phone beat into my head and I picked it up and it was Lewis.

'I'm just calling about the violin,' he said, and my mouth went dry when I heard the uncharacteristic edge in his voice. 'Where did you say you picked it up?'

'Don't joke with me, now, Lewis,' I croaked. 'I'm skint.'

'I'm serious. I'm getting a bloke to come and look at it in an hour, but the shop's in a bit of an uproar, let me tell you. Mate, you should take out a ticket in the lottery.'

I gripped the phone. 'What are you saying? What's the violin worth?'

He laughed. 'The violin? Nothing, mate. It's a piece of crap. Worth about twenty bucks.'

There was a pause.

'I'm talking about the bow.'

'You've lost me.'

'The bow. The violin bow that came in the case. When I saw the inlay I knew you had something there, but I had to check with the Conservatorium to make sure.' He mentioned a foreign name that sounded like a brand of expensive vodka. 'What I can't understand is how it ended up at Camberwell market.'

'What's it worth?' I interrupted him. And I was tensing my stomach, ready for the blow, almost expecting it now.

'I'd say around $700,' said Lewis.

Later, eating a crumpet and looking down at the city of Vienna, I notice the piece of jigsaw I thought was missing is in fact hidden under the ashtray. I just couldn't see it for looking.

I slide it out and fit it into place, feeling the whole configuration resist, and move slightly out of skew. I move it back with the flat of my hand, feeling it shift. Strengthen. Interlock.

Soundtrack

Rachel is cooking cauliflower cheese when her daughter tells her she has joined a band and they will be practising in the rumpus room starting next Saturday. Rachel leaves off stirring the white sauce and turns to look at her daughter incredulously.

Emma is slumping in the doorway wearing the look of tired defiance she wore the day she got the tattoo. Rachel burst into tears that day, not because the tattoo was bleeding or defacing or even offensive — a Celtic cross surrounding a yin-yang symbol just above her breast — but because she was transported in a moment to a day seventeen years before when she had tickled that plump, powdered body, kissed it noisily just where the yin yang now twisted. Yin and yang, the flux of being: the irony of this is not lost on Rachel, who was a child in the 1960s and by the 1970s hung a batik sarong featuring this very symbol as a curtain in her doorway in the old house in Cardigan Street she shared with seven others. But now she is thirty-eight and grating cheese for dinner, thinking she can live with her daughter's tattoo and even the navel ring and boots, but she has heard the music Emma listens to and does not want it punctuating her Saturdays. Emma is not asking, though; she is informing. Where does a seventeen-year-old get so much certainty?

Rachel feels winded—tossed in front of a camera and told to act, the only person without a script and in someone else's costume. She has been feeling lately, in fact, that her life has a kind of soundtrack. Sometimes she can almost hear it: a melancholy instrumental as she stirs sauce, a frenetic salsa as she runs round in the morning like a cartoon, clashing foreboding cymbals as her daughter drops a bombshell. Soundtrack when she finds the battery in the Datsun is flat and hits her head dully, theatrically, on the steering wheel. Soundtrack as she stares at her reflection in the bathroom. The film and the score of the film that seem to compose the key scenes of her life are driving her crazy.

Mirror shot, something authoritative says in her head as she scrutinises the lines under her eyes before she goes to bed. *Pan around as she touches her face and reaches for moisturiser and ... cut.* There is a kind of a Richard Clayderman piano number swelling in the background. The scene spins, fades, some audience somewhere applauds, some director is a contender for an award.

Now, as she grates, she tries to stem the tide rattling away in her head, describing her movements shot by shot, she tries to actually clear a space to think, to put her case to Emma. But the babbling continues: *Close-up as she grates.*

Cut to her face struggling with emotion. Cue soundtrack, cello solo.

Rachel's mouth opens and closes, as if waiting for its lines. She is losing the trick of improvisation. She grates the cheese down to a nub as Emma tells her there are only four people in the band and that they are called Melting Carpet. Rachel, with a large, disassociated part of her brain, musing like a bewildered spectator, wonders if the problem is television.

Rachel's husband Jerry still sports the ponytail he wore to Sunbury '74, and he is still a sweet man who wants a Harley. When Emma's friends come over, he often tells them he once played blues harmonica with Max Merritt and the Meteors. Jerry thinks the group may have had a revival recently, like so many other bands of his era. He lets Emma's friends play his Jimi Hendrix LPs, eagerly showing them how to lower the stylus. Rachel, watching, can't believe that fate has bounced like this and they like Jimi Hendrix. She can't believe she lives in a world where her own child doesn't know how to play a record. *Everything*, Rachel thinks, *is going too fast.* On bad days she looks askance at Jerry and Emma together, wonders if they could perhaps have been sent from a casting agency, derides the big clumsy strokes this script seems to be written in and contemplates what might yet be getting drowned out in the noise. *'Scuse me*, she drones to herself, *while I kiss this guy.*

Jerry had wanted Emma to be a home birth, in their large, airy bedroom in Warburton. He would have received her into his big hands saying 'Unbelievable' and 'This is blowing me away'. He would have wrapped her in the sarong with the yin and yang symbol, pulled from the door and given a quick shake. He would have had Brian Eno on the stereo, thinks Rachel. Back then, that would have been the soundtrack. She hesitates, remembering the hospital birth, Jerry indignantly telling the nurses that they weren't wrapping his daughter in alfoil, no way. What had the cleaners been singing as they hauled the industrial polishers up and down those corridors outside her room? Streisand oozing that she was a woman in love. Rachel, her world collapsed into baby adoration, had absorbed all those lyrics as if by osmosis, and agreed.

Rachel has just discovered she is pregnant again. She wonders what Jerry will say now, and what he might put on the stereo this time. The news has hit her like a stun-gun. It is a twist to the plot she would never have dreamed of. Even now, three days after receiving the results, listening to Jerry trying to sing along to Powderfinger in the lounge room, to Emma describing the musical ambitions of Melting Carpet, watching something as ordinary as cheese melting under the griller, Rachel finds she has to push herself off from the profound edge of disbelief into the far shallows where such ideas might be viewed from a sane and manageable distance. Rachel's mind paddles this way and that, trying to encompass the idea of pregnancy. Faintly across the water comes music; the string section swells as she floats at the far side of possibility. She hears ethereal voices sing: *Out of the blue, you came out of the blue.* She can't decide whether it's something her subconscious has invented, or whether it's Burt Bacharach.

'You're having me on,' says Jerry the following Saturday. He is washing the dog under the hose, and straightens up staring at her.

Rachel says, 'Are you happy or not?'

They seem to be floundering with the dialogue; she wants to cut and do the scene again. *Slow pan around the two figures*, chatters the voice in her head, *followed by close-up of husband running a soapy hand through his hair in a gesture of amazement. Close-up of wife's face as she tries to form the words: 'We don't have to have it.' Long overhead shot of the back garden.*

The soundtrack to this confrontation is Melting Carpet, who pound from the back of the house, the same four bars over and over.

Jerry jumps up to hug her. 'Wow,' he says. Rachel is trying to imagine him with a baby papoose, a baby inside pulling his ponytail done up with a scrunchie. She thinks about disposable nappies, Emma's friends, another eighteen years of running to salsa music every morning, her back as she hauls a two-year-old out of the car seat. And the money—my God. Seconds pass in these flash forwards, tiny zippy scenes Rachel fleshes out with a few moments of dialogue: presents under the Christmas tree, parent–teacher nights, going grey, the bathroom mirror scene repeated for ironic emphasis. She focuses on the dog lowering its head to bite the water flowing from the end of the dropped hose, strains to hear the soundtrack.

'I think I want it,' she says.

'Whoa, it's just kind of hard to get your head around,' says sweet, ingenuous Jerry, just as he had done seventeen years ago.

'Better to burn out and die young,' howl Melting Carpet, 'that's what Kurt said before he ate his gun.' Rachel, vacuuming, wonders if she has heard the lyrics right. The bass player in the band has a stud through his tongue, and Rachel thinks she might have got off lightly with the yin-yang tattoo. Emma had stared open-mouthed at the news her parents had conceived a baby, then stormed out saying, 'That is so gross.' Rachel knows she is embarrassed, confused, perhaps threatened. She has read comforting analyses of this in library books. But when Emma screamed that she was moving out as soon as she turned eighteen, and her friends would look at her now like she was some kind of freak, probably, Rachel had found herself screaming back: 'Good! Go!'

'I hate you!' Emma had yelled.

Music like heavy metal had filled Rachel's ears, discordant noises full of ear-splitting feedback that made her wince and want to cover her head.

Now Emma is talking with studied carelessness about group houses, about moving in with the band, who sit at Rachel's kitchen table and eat whole cakes slice by slice and giggle uncontrollably. Rachel pictures the batik door hangings, the Kashmir Musk incense, the rattan matting of her own group houses, and doubts anything she can imagine will resemble the household Emma is planning.

The leather jackets of the band members look like some child has been firing at them with a pop riveter. Now Emma is playing the drums; she can hear her, it sounds enraged. *Where does all that rage come from?* wonders Rachel, remembering the meditation tapes and restful dolphin–rainbow mobiles of Emma's babyhood. Massage for your baby. A piece of amber on a leather thong around that chubby, adorable neck, which today sports a livid lovebite covered with pale foundation. Melting Carpet has a gig, at the High School Students Only Rage. They have taken on a keyboard player because his father has a kombivan and can lend it to haul their gear. Jerry has offered to do the sound mixing, news greeted with suppressed, stoned hysteria by the band. Rachel is now five-months pregnant. Her condition has given her vagueness and detached dreaminess a force and a shape. She hears vintage Paul Simon as she walks in the park each morning, sometimes a touch of Vivaldi's *Four Seasons*.

She clings to the soundtrack, conscious that it gives things form; it lets her settle back in the audience and be carried along. *Still crazy ... after all these years ...* she hums along to herself, pensively viewing a long camera angle of herself kicking up leaves, soft-focused and waiting for the next cue. She looks at baby photos of Emma and thinks: *no bikinis without sunscreen, ever again* and *look at that, not even a hat* and *a piece of Amazon rainforest the size of a football field disappearing every minute.* She watches the real-life cop shows and shakes her head in horror. *What sort of a world*, she thinks, and *I'll be fifty-nine at its twenty-first birthday party* and *how are we ever going to get enough sleep?* She sees Jerry in a misty, future dream he has long held of motorbiking around Australia, both of them, and the soundtrack washes sadly over the filter effects. Impossible now. She almost hears the lyrics whispered, sees a tiny speeded-up video clip of Jerry selling his acoustic guitar, walking away to a lonesome Nashville instrumental solo. She reads in the paper of abducted children, children playing with computer pets, children going on diets at age eight. *Things are out of control*, thinks Rachel. *They are awesome. They are so hard to get your head around.*

When Rachel goes into labour Jerry is not home. She eyes her overnight bag carefully packed by the front door, her vision grey around the edges, sweat springing on her forehead. *I've changed my mind*, she thinks as her waters break. She doubles over the table—*zoom in for a close-up on the wedding ring*—her hands flat down in front of her. *Jesus, have I changed my mind.* Her own breath sucks in and comes out a yell. It's not a cry, thinks Rachel from a new abstract eyrie, not a moan, a whimper, a feeble call. With each breath, another yell comes, unpretty and shocking in the silence of the kitchen, and brings Emma running to stare horrified from the doorway. Rachel hears white noise, background hiss, the stylus caught in the last empty grooves of the record, and nothing more to hum along to.

As she sinks deeper and deeper into what her own

body is engineering, Rachel feels herself in bed, comes up for air to hear the bedroom phone extension snickering as someone dials out. Emma, Emma. Three calls. Rachel thinks about sinking, the going under in surrender, opening your mouth to water. She surfaces to gulp great lungfuls of air, knowing that the ambulance is not going to get here in time, knowing her husband, who she suddenly wants very much, is somewhere stuck in traffic. She feels transition start and recalls the barked instructions of the on-duty obstetrician she had recoiled from in her other labour, who had turned around and hissed Jerry out of the way, and Jerry's hoarse, humble assent which had made tears spring in her eyes. *It's going to be here*, Rachel thinks, and everything crowding up the airwaves stops suddenly to listen as she twists the Guatemalan quilt in both her hands and sets her jaw. *Here and now, then*, she thinks. *Come on, then.*

'Up,' says a voice, pushing pillows behind her back, and she's confusing it with those nurses, the one with the chewing gum who did the rounds in her brand new Sony Walkman, bringing Rachel magazines. Rachel's hand goes out gesturing for the mask, for nitrous oxide, and knocks both the digital clock and the bedside lamp off the table. *Without time, without light*, thinks Rachel, *and I'm going to die now.*

'Here,' says the voice, and puts a straw between her lips, and Rachel sucks apple juice like it is ambrosia, hears weeping that is not her own, and is enfolded in patchouli-scented arms which hold her still, slow her down.

Then as her second daughter is born, she sees through a

blur of tears only the beloved, holy skin of her first—close, close to her and sheened with sweat; she is eye to eye with a never-ending Celtic twist, two fish tumbling forever in the struggling, messy flux of life. *It is not quiet, it is never quiet*, thinks Rachel, feeling the head crown, a leg jump with anticipation. *It is not a meditation, that is a lie.* At some point she senses Jerry there, she hears Jerry say that it is awesome. And Rachel thinks: *Yes.*

'Hey, Mum. Watch this.' Emma gives the baby a wooden spoon. Rachel gazes on that new body, that unsullied flesh free of tattoos, studs, scars and piercings, dings, bruises, inoculation and stretch marks. *Just wait*, she thinks tranquilly, holding those kicking, uncalloused feet.

Jerry, up all night, has spent the morning playing a selection of records, making a bedtime tape—Jefferson Airplane, The Mamas and the Papas, Queen and Bananas in Pyjamas. The room has crashed to *Bohemian Rhapsody*. Now it is silent. Rachel listens but can hear nothing, stands gazing at the astonishing, abrupt fact of the baby before her.

'She looks like the Dalai Lama,' says Emma, 'only new.'

The baby grapples with the wooden spoon's handle with industrious concentration, waves it gently, staring gravely at her observers, her small, devoted audience.

'Look,' says Rachel. 'She's conducting.'

Take me anywhere, she prays silently and fiercely into the invisible music. *Take me anywhere at all.*

Direct Action

Direct action. You don't want to hear it. You want to make another pot of tea, and wait for *Star Trek: The Next Generation* to come on. Direct action means arguing with punters on the street who try to pull your placards off you, and dancing round the missile base so that the cops can laugh themselves sick before they move in on you. It's something you admire hearing about second-hand, shaking your head at someone else's bruises. It's not something you feel like doing, on a cold winter's night after dinner. Except that you can't stop thinking that right now, after dinner or not, and all through tonight, and tomorrow, twenty-four hours a day, in fact, seven days a week, Barron Paper Mills, just up the road, are glugging industrial effluent straight into the river.

Picketing? The laundry is full of pickets. STOP TOXIC SPILL, they say. THE PLANET IS NOT YOUR TOILET. And so on. Barron executives, accustomed to paying big dollars to give toilet paper a good image, have an Environmental Impact

Study saying that the effluent falls within acceptable levels of toxic contamination. Life seems full of acceptable levels now. I myself fall into the acceptable level of thirteen per cent of qualified tradespeople unable to find employment. I've stood knee-deep in the sludge twenty metres down from the dual-emission outlet pipes and been asked by well-pressed retirees just off to the pokies why I haven't got a job. *Because they've closed. They laid me off. I worked for four years, let me show you my certificate and union card.* No point screaming. No point even answering. There's a photo of us 'Direct Action' campaigners, cut out of the local rag and brown and oil-splattered now, on the fridge. We look puny and pale in our rolled-up jeans, holding dead fish, and every time I pass it I can't help cringing at the headline 'Ecowarriors'—saving the public the trouble of jeering at us by doing it myself.

I observe the comforting sight of the Enterprise going where no one has gone before (used to be no *man* but see how non-sexism has changed the world), sip my tea and watch Riker dispensing Klingons. Glug, glug, goes the effluent two kilometres away, unstoppable, poisonous, irreversible. This time of night it slows to a trickle, by 9.30 in the morning it's like the North Sea pipeline.

'I'm providing jobs,' the executive from Barron had argued with me as I stood in the river that morning, knowing where to hit the nerve. I had an answer ready but couldn't trust my voice, or my hand holding the rotting fish. He'd sneered at my 'Vegetarians of the World Unite' T-shirt.

'Sure you've got your priorities straight, son?' he'd said, and when I still didn't answer, he'd said, 'Come on, speak up, moron', and I'd thrown the fish, and there'd been trouble.

Sometimes Monday mornings I still jump awake at 6.45 and go to roll out of bed before realising there's no whistle to get up for. It'd be a long bike ride to work anyway, even if I'd kept my job, since the factory is now in Macau. Some other poor bastard's starting up the oxytorch now, checking his mask and checking his back. People used to ask for me at the workshop. 'Get a skill and you'll always be in demand,' is something my Dad used to say, and he believed it too, until they retired him. He says he doesn't miss the work. Tells me this in the middle of his shed, which has more tools in it than Mitre 10. His face lighting up when a neighbour brings their car over, hurrying for a spanner, telling them it's no trouble.

'Cheer up, Gaz,' is what he says now. 'It's not you, son. There'll be an opening for a skilled bloke sooner or later.'

I have a plan. My only visible direct action thus far is stepping for the first time in fourteen years into a butcher shop. Two dollars' worth of bones, paper bag please, not plastic. I go every day for two weeks. The butcher becomes my friend. All day he bashes up the carcasses of dead things, and I've never seen the smile off his face. Now there's a puzzle for you.

'Dad,' I say, 'I need to borrow the oxy.'

His face brightens. He heaves himself off the Recliner

Rocker. 'Got a job on, son?'

'Kind of.'

'That's the way.' He pads out to the shed, checks the set in the box.

'You wouldn't have a few bits of steel plate lying around, would you?'

'How big?'

I indicate with my hands.

He stops, thinks. 'I just might, out the back.'

My dad, recycler since 1963. He returns, his arms weighted.

'You could patch a hole on the *Queen Mary* with these.'

'Just about.'

'Hang about while I get you a couple of welding rods.'

He putters about, putting his hand on everything he wants, competent, cheerful. He would have had fifteen years more productive time in him at the garage, given a chance. He could have trained the apprentice who replaced him. Now he is on the scrapheap, and his response is to make something useful with the scrap.

'I think the bottle's pretty full,' he says, checking it.

'Great. Thanks.'

'Good on yer, Gary. It's like I told you—there's always an opening for a bloke with skills.'

'One or two, still,' I say, hefting the box.

And I'm almost at the door before he says in a voice just a degree or two cooler, 'So, what's the job, then?'

Sprung, I turn around and walk back.

'Remember that time we went fishing in the Hootie?'

'Sure I do.' He's fiddling with the welding rod, putting it into the vice, turning the handle. Listening.

'Remember when I caught that brown trout?'

There are things I hope my father remembers from my childhood; about three big things. One was the day he pushed me off, minus training wheels, on my first two-wheeler — a low-slung green dragster — and suddenly I was steering and pedalling and the bike was staying upright, and I sneaked a quick look behind me and my dad was jumping down the track, punching the air with triumph. Another time was when I'd fixed a tiny leak in our Clarke's backyard swimming pool with my bike repair kit. My father had taken a few short steps towards the repair, stopped, considered, and looked at me with what an eight-year-old boy could only take for respect.

And, last of all, in lit-up focus in my memory, there was the fishing. Me with my rod from Santa, my father with an old rubber lure designed to catch a fourteen-pound Murray cod on the South Australian rivers in the 1950s. Did I tell you he never threw anything away?

We had been fishing for an hour, not saying anything, when there was a bang on my rod like a bailiff's knock and the K-mart plastic bent like a horseshoe and my father whooped with sudden childlike excitement. His hands flew out to grab the rod, then slowly went back into his pockets, where they rolled and twitched as he instructed me how to reel the fish in, his teeth clenched. It was a big brown trout, just about the most beautiful thing I'd ever seen, and my father's 'you little *beauty*' fell on my head like a benediction.

The trout lay there drowning in the air, and I could see the miraculous gills opening and closing, its eyes moving as it gulped the wrong element, two old scars on its big mottled back, and then everything slowed down and I reached my fingers, fumbling with agonised realisation, into the trout's mouth to get that hook out, and I snatched the fish up in both hands and threw it back into the water. The absolutely silent moments when it was flexing and shining in the air over the brown water lasted for years, and while I waited for it to hit I felt something come loose in my chest, emerge, test the air and flap away in big white beats.

I want my father to remember this day, the last day I ever fished.

'There aren't any brown trout in the Hootie now, Dad.'

He examines the edge on a chisel, rubs it up and down a scar on his thumb. 'There's not much of anything any more, son. Not that kind of thing.'

'They're pouring emission straight into the water down there, from two pipes hanging out over the bank.'

He tests the chisel, nodding slowly as he works out what I want his welding gear for. 'They're pouring human shit straight into the ocean, too,' he says, pinning me with a glance, 'but I haven't noticed you welding your arse shut.'

The moment twists in the air, seconds away from the wet smack of too late.

'If you're not going to lend it to me, just say.'

He slides the chisel carefully back into its slot in his

box. Sighs. Fumbles for the metre to check the levels in the acetylene tank.

Rome was attacked by Gallic troops in 390 BC and what raised the alarm that saved the city? Geese. The holy geese in the city's temple started up and the invaders couldn't quieten them and Rome woke up to itself. I read this in an article titled 'Microlivestock: Little-known Small Animals with a Promising Economic Future', along with the information that geese are used now to guard missile bases in Europe. Geese. They just raise the alarm and gabble away and don't shut up, and you would be mistaken if you didn't take that seriously, standing there with your sabotage tools and camouflage gear on. This is the kind of information I would never have learned about in my old job. You get a fair bit of reading in when you're unemployed.

Barron's four German Shepherds bounce down to the fence when they see me, the bringer of midnight snacks for two weeks. Barron Paper Mills has made two great mistakes in the protection of its plant. One, it has installed dogs of a famously aggressive breed, but it has neglected to train them because it thinks their presence is a deterrent in itself. Two, they have fed these dogs on dry dog-kibble and water. The first night I pushed four kilos of lamb shanks through the wire, the dogs' barking switched off like someone had pulled the plug. They glanced up at me as they dropped their heads to it with a look so sentient, so conspiratorial, it was breathtaking. One of them, I swear, winked.

Fourteen nights later, our transaction is as businesslike as a drug deal. Through the cyclone-wire mesh goes eight kilos of beef ribs sliced up on the butcher's bandsaw. Inside the nightwatchman's room, the guard sleeps through *Letterman*. The bark of the dogs would wake him. But the dogs don't bark. They're dumb, but not that dumb. They give me quick leery dog smiles. I am Dog Santa. Then they barrel off into the darkness, meat and drool trailing from their mouths. I cut the wire close to a pole, where the flap snaps back invisibly. Barron, you should have invested in geese.

As I move just inside the lights on the fence perimeters, behind the factory towards the pipeline, I'm thinking of my father's hands, pushed down into his pockets like he was holding down foam buoys, clenching and jumping in there, torn between taking something and giving it away. The fingers that could reach in behind a spinning fanbelt and locate a nut and adjust it precisely. My own hands that used to be hard with a smattering of burns and marks but now are soft, with clean fingernails. Want to know what someone does for a living, check their hands. Hold out yours, shake theirs, and you'll know everything you need to know. I'm puffing, out of condition, fingers tired already from just cutting the wire. Watch out world, here comes Mr Activist.

Hoisting myself down through blackberries to the pipes, I breathe easier now, 150 metres from the building. The oxy, when I light it, sounds a solid hiss of hot energy, like a gas lamp out in the bush—loud as a roar, it seems to me. I turn the flame, pull down my mask. It smells like an honest day's work, a smell I haven't quite forgotten yet.

It takes me an hour, but I was never one to rush a job. I lean into the blackberries, my boot wedged into poisoned riverbank. Those radiant blue chips waterfall off the metal like the fireworks we used to nail to the fence back before you needed to be a qualified pyrotechnician to handle them. Catherine wheels, spinning molten stars, my mum lighting the whole packet, every one different.

My back starts to protest and the scratches down my legs smoulder. I know what I'm doing, though. I'm welding metal together, watching the solder grey and cool in a neat permanent join even as I move to the next section, twisted around a waste pipe in the darkness, hearing the liquid inside sizzle against the heat as the pipe fills slowly, finishing off the second plate, hunched against a riverbank I once caught a fish off. By tomorrow morning, the guy I threw the fish at will crank up his machinery and things will slowly seize in a white-hot and expensive flooding. His ruined two-hundred-dollar shoes will splash him out of the swill, into head office to call the police.

Stepping back now around the manicured grass, every second expecting the sliding blue and red lights of a cop car and the android crackle of their voices over the radios to greet me at the road, I swallow nothing again and again. The taste of nickel, of smoking solder in my mouth. But there is just the night there, grey and woolly and incomprehensible like I've just woken up into it. I'm still wearing my welding mask, hobbling as the muscles in my legs start stiffening up. The dogs, breathing meaty breath onto me, fawn around, coming out of the darkness and leaping up at me, their brains addled with protein and low-IQ self-interest. I am covered with oily sludge from the emission pipes, and saliva from the sated dogs.

Barron, neglecting dog training, did however splash out on surveillance cameras. As I unwittingly pass one's red-eyed field of vision I am thinking only of getting home. But two days later in the paper there is a blurry photo of something that looks like Bigfoot under a story in which Barron executives cite figures that they say have cost the whole community dearly. Mindless and malicious sabotage that affects the reputation of Australian business both at home and abroad. They cite their Environmental Impact Study, their acceptable levels, their state-of-the-art corporate workplace agreement policies.

The cops take one look at the job, and start looking for welders with a history of disturbing the peace.

It's a small field of contenders, and it doesn't take them long.

They have the photo when they come over to my place, and one of them looks at it and gives a little smile at the blurry figure emerging out of the dark in the big, black welding mask, both hands raised and holding cylinders. I know what he is thinking. The resemblance has struck me, too.

'Stand and deliver, eh?' he says to me, and we both grin. He's the kind of bloke I'd buy a beer.

'Tell 'em I died game,' I say. I get a ride in a police car for my trouble.

Outside the court, what the press is fond of calling a small but vocal group of protestors has assembled, and the posters out of the laundry are in action again. There is ragged cheering as I make my way through.

There have been questions, which Barron's media releases have answered with an increasing note of self-righteousness. The press aren't given a gift like this—a toilet-paper manufacturer—every day, and they don't waste it. There are also headlines in the 'Something Fishy?' vein, showing journalists frowning thoughtfully at a high-tide mark of solid scum. Barron execs have posed nervously for photos around the new pipes with filter attachments and released their sudden altruistic intention to create a waterbird sanctuary upstream, but their spin doctors, deep into damage control, have kicked a bit of an own goal with their new slogan.

'We're here to clean up!' doesn't do them any favours at all.

Me, I am dubbed 'The Man of Steel'. I am in the Odd Spot.

'Name?' I am asked in the courtroom.

'Gary Sutherland.'

'And your profession?'

'Welder.'

The prosecutor gives me a *now-come-on* look. 'Wouldn't it be more correct to say you are unemployed?'

'Yes, I am unemployed.'

'And have been on unemployment benefits for well over two years?'

It's funny, but I'm not even angry. 'It would be more correct to say I am a qualified welder,' I say, 'who does not have a job.'

As they read the charge, the noise outside increases into one of those clapping call-and-response chants. From inside it sounds a bit like a herd of distant honking, just between you and me. I smile.

The river doesn't look any cleaner. Some days green algae makes it look solid as a billiard table; some days it's black as Ned Kelly's eyes. There will still never be any fish in it. That part of our lives is over, mostly. This is what occurs to me as I am charged that day in court: that there aren't enough moments of fumbling to pull out the hook, our hands no longer move independently of our heads. But as I walk out, I catch sight of my father, down the back, head up, worth ten of the bastards in suits. The look he has in his eye is not the one he had when I caught the fish.

It is the look he had when I let the fish go.

The Correct Names of Things

All the time I worked at Eddie Lim's café, I never once saw him or any of the other kitchenhands eat Chinese food. When 11.00 p.m. rolled around they went and got hamburgers, and ate them sitting in the greasy wreckage of the kitchen, staring into nothing, and chewing. Overlaying everything else would come the smell of hot cardboard, wilted french fries. After clean-up they would play cards till dawn.

'Hey, Ellen!' Eddie would shout. 'What you want?'

I would pause from scraping plates, and think about the menu in its oily plastic cover, the food customers had been buying all night: glistening chunks of spare ribs, chicken, pineapple.

'Nothing, Eddie. Thanks.'

'You gotta have *some*thing!' His face, round as a dumpling, blinks reproachfully—Jackie Chan in a big, crumpled apron. 'Wonton soup? Whaddayou say, huh?'

Later when I go home I will pull my shirt over my head and smell a gust of sweet and sour sauce. My hair hangs limp with cooking fat. In the afternoons, before the dinner rush, I like to watch Joey boil the chickens, strip off the skin like a steaming, waxy rubber glove, and cut it up for spring rolls. The flesh is torn up for chop suey and the feet and head go back into the pot for soup stock. Joey's wrist flicking in a measure of monosodium glutamate, catching the drip on the lip of the pot, tossing the wok so that everything inside rolls over like a wave on a smoking black beach is worth watching. When the dining room is set up I help him prep. Spring rolls, he tells me as I stand alongside him wrapping, should be tight as cigarettes. I laugh and agree, saying mine look more like soggy cabbage wrapped up in a serviette. We say all this with a mixture of fifteen English words and elaborate mime. Joey is a refugee, with the same shock of hair as the suspect shot by the South Vietnamese general in that famous piece of war footage, the same neat checked shirt. Now he drives a rusting old Falcon station wagon, small and precise as a child at the wheel, and makes Chinese food. When he cuts vegetables, he sets the cleaver against the tip then the first knuckle, then the second knuckle of his left forefinger, the cleaver blurring and deadly, every piece of carrot precisely the same. At times like this, watching the calm, relaxed planes of his face, I wish I spoke whatever language he is thinking in.

'You no like my food, Ellen?' Eddie is pretending to be hurt, now. He sits on the high stool at the takeaway counter. 'You take these instead.' He hands me a plastic bag of fortune cookies. 'Maybe you get a good fortune and marry that boyfriend and have babies.'

'Eddie, I'm too young!' I put the cookies in my bag. This happens every Friday night. At home, I have a container full of prophecies and aphorisms, tiny slips of waxed paper with blue words advising me to turn catastrophe into opportunity, to eat well and make my peace before going into battle.

'Anyway,' I say, 'I notice you guys aren't eating anything off the menu.'

Eddie's sweet pork-bun face creases in delight.

'No ...' he says, fumbling under his grease-stiff apron for cigarettes. 'We only like *Chinese* food.'

He cracks up laughing at himself, cackling as he turns the 'Open' sign around. Now he will wash up. Then he'll store what's left in the refrigerator, wipe the benches down, take out the roll of money he's made tonight, and cut the cards.

It is 1981 and I make $23.50 a night. Upstairs from the restaurant is a discreet brothel and at 10.30 p.m. someone always comes down to pick up some takeaway. The women look tired, like any other shiftworker, sick of spraying their hair, bored but not really hungry. One of them is only seventeen, three years younger than me, and when she comes down she orders a batch of caramelised apples. She has a sweet tooth, and a vague air of being elsewhere, and she seems always just out of the shower. The other women tell me that that's what she does. She showers and men pay to watch her. Amazed, I watch those men arrive and slip upstairs as the night progresses. Some of them are wearing jogging gear, some tie up a dog to the post outside. All night as I pack and add up and ask if people want forks or chopsticks, I am thinking of her, drying herself and getting back into the shower, over and over. Dreamily, I stare at Joey's hands guiding the cleaver, that repeated, precise bending of the finger, shaving so close to catastrophe and blood.

My boyfriend is studying marine biology, and wants to change to economics/law. In 1981 you can contemplate things like this, because education is free and the university is full of people on a kind of long, messy postponement, swapping courses midstream like trying on clothes. I am enrolled in a bachelor's degree in Russian literature, and under the takeaway counter is a copy of Gogol's *Dead Souls*. My boyfriend often turns up at my place in the middle of the night. He likes to go and see bands; he considers punk rock an omen of social anarchy. He crawls into bed smelling of rum and a deep, bitter cloud of cigarette smoke, crunching fortune cookies. Jangling energy seems to ring off him, as if decibels of music are leaking from his skin. '*Things are rarely what they seem*,' he whispers, reading the blue words, and then: 'A tall, dark stranger may well slip into your bed. You would be unwise to refuse him.'

He laughs at himself, twitching, humming, manic. I try to imagine him as an economist or lawyer. I can't imagine him as anything other than what he is: twenty years old and in a perpetual state of pleasing himself.

'Sweet and sour pork!' Eddie echoes me. 'Lemon chicken! Large fried rice! Gotcha!' As he rattles back the order for Chinese food Chinese people would never eat, his accent takes the words and chops the consonants, makes them one-syllable Chinese again. 'Swee sou' po'! Spri' ro'!'

After hours, I practise this cartoonish delivery at Eddie's request. 'Shor sou'!' I cry. 'Lar' fry rie!'

'See? So easy to speak Chinese!' cackles Eddie as he scrubs the bench, having to wipe tears of hilarity from his heavy-lidded eyes. Composing himself with a sigh, he collects all the receipts and stuffs them up on the shelf where he stores tins of soup that nobody ever orders, that are covered with a patina of dust and oil. Shark Fin Soup. Bird's Nest Soup. They are not on the menu. Four soups are served at the café, and they are all ladled from the same pot, rendered down from chicken feet and necks. I clean up splattered soy sauce and think of what my boyfriend has told me about sharks. 'No bones,' he'd said. 'Only cartilage. So there's no skeletonic remains so that scientists can carbon date how long sharks have been on the planet.'

Sceptically, I'd asked: 'What about teeth?'

'That's the freaky bit. Their teeth are constantly falling out and being replaced so that we can't even tell how old individual sharks get. They could live for hundreds of years, for all we know.' This was at the beginning of his marine biology course last year, when he was still interested and his tutor apparently hadn't taken a dislike to him, when he still talked of us going up to Cairns and getting our scuba-diving certificates. 'We should keep a shark in captivity for years and years,' he'd said, grinning, 'just to watch the bastard age.'

All that bone-free shark to eat, I used to think, and the Chinese make a soup out of the fin, of cartilage and grey skin. Or not a bird or an egg, but a bird's nest. That was before I watched them cook, and learned they wasted nothing, that they shaved a piece of beef so thin it was almost transparent, that they filled rice paper with chicken skin and cabbage and could roll it up as tightly as a cigarette. I made the mistake, too, of thinking their gambling was reckless, that maybe they were betting for fun.

During the week, I go to lectures, I attend my tutorials in small carpeted tutors' rooms lined with books. I am two months away from graduating, I have been asked to consider honours the following year, there are rumours of tutoring positions. I picture a room like this, branches knocking at the window, surreptitious reading all day, a swivel chair. The air conditioner hums discreetly. It is the beginning of the 1980s, and the university has money and it wants women—on its staff, on its committees, on its books.

'The world is your oyster,' says the Dean when he sees us. We are nearly all women, in Literature. The boys have finished with Arts, they have discarded Humanities and are ready for the new toys now: computer science and economics, ready to claim the decade ahead. Predatory and boneless, my boyfriend is drifting along there with them, moving on a tide and ever alert to the main chance, unable to stay still.

You will soon discover wealth, I read as I eat fortune cookies and watch the midnight movie. *The brave must grasp the dragon's tail. What is most valuable we cannot count.* Almond and egg flavour crumbles on my tongue. Tonight two little children were sitting in the café when I arrived, doing their homework at the corner table. They were half-Chinese, polite and excited, jumping up to glimpse through the servery and hovering round the swing door.

'Finish your homework,' Eddie had said sternly. 'My kids,' he'd added to me in explanation.

The children smile at me sweetly. I gape to encompass the sudden idea of Eddie with a Caucasian wife, and he shrugs.

'Didn't work out,' he says. 'She says I can have them for this weekend. Sit down and do your homework!' he repeats to the children. They return to the table, obedient and whispering. He brings out a plate of prawn crackers and puts it down in front of them without a word. As he hastens back to the kitchen, I see tears deep in the creases of his blinking eyes. The other kitchenhands busy themselves with chopping. It's like being shown the back of a photograph—lines and lines of mysterious text about something you assumed was simple.

I dip prawns in cornflour paste, breadcrumb them, slide them into oil. Joey sharpens a cleaver, sniffing with a cold, singing phonetic Bee Gees to himself. On the counter are twenty-five separate containers each holding one ingredient. A day to shop, a day to chop, Eddie tells me, smacking a knife into piles of cabbage. Four weeks and I will graduate with distinctions, three more essays including my masterly piece on *Dead Souls*. I will have a degree from an institution dedicated to the pursuit of pure knowledge, which has intimated it may have a place for me. My boyfriend is restless with a nihilism I don't have the experience yet to recognise as selfishness, that I misinterpret as something deep and attractively Russian.

Suddenly a man appears outside and sets up an aluminium ladder against the wall of the restaurant. In his hands he carries a huge pair of wire cutters.

'What's that bastard doing?' cries Eddie Lim. I go outside and ask. The man says he is cutting the restaurant's electricity supply. Eddie is a delinquent client with a three-month outstanding bill. Eddie's restaurant is about to go broke. His face is trying to be expressionless as he says this, but he cannot prevent a slick grin sliding across it as he hands me a card.

'Tell the Chink,' he says.

'Wait, we have customers, we cooking right now,' says Eddie, appearing, but he feels the man's sly pleasure and is abashed by it. It isn't until he fumbles under his apron, scarlet with shame, hunting for his betting roll, that the man lowers the wire cutters and snorts with contempt. Customers inside pause over their soup, watching.

'Wait,' says Eddie. 'Please.' His face is as boxed as when he watches the cards fall. He takes out his cheap cigarettes and holds the crumpled packet carefully in his left hand, still digging. In his right hand, when he withdraws it again, is a box of matches, a few folded notes, a scrap of white paper with figures on it. He blinks, defeated. Down the steps comes the seventeen-year-old girl from the brothel, slowly and coolly folding her arms as she stands at the base of the ladder.

'What's the problem here?' she says, and I feel a sudden intense change, the two men seem to lean towards her, her lazy adolescent certainty speaks a language to them that streams straight past me. She shifts her weight to her other leg like something underwater changing direction, and looks steadily up at the man from the electricity company on the ladder, and under her gaze he descends like someone suffering vertigo.

'No problem,' he says, and I can tell there won't be. Back inside, I roll chopsticks inside paper serviettes, thinking that I am twenty years old and the owner of 145 pieces of Confucian advice and I know nothing at all. That night as I'm packing to go, Eddie and Joey sit on the floor in the kitchen shuffling cards, shuffling debts and alimony and war and missing relatives and proceeds from thirteen straight hours' work in a dead suburban shopping mall. I know nothing.

'Have a think over the holidays,' the Dean says. 'The option's there.' At home in my flat it spreads itself out like a logical road map where you follow directions from here to there and end up tenured, making money talking about words, opening books whose significant passages have been underlined and trammelled into elegant arguments lasting years. 'The pursuit of knowledge is an admirable thing,' says the Dean, and then, 'There are plenty of worse jobs,' smiling with a lame attempt at mateyness. My boyfriend fails three subjects and launches into an assessment appeal with more energy than he's devoted to two years of study, and in February gets busted and charged for selling hash to an undercover narcotics agent at a thrash gig at the uni bar.

Stare calmly in the eye of adversity, bow like a reed. On a hot, still evening at the end of summer, I unroll one that says: *The root of true wisdom lies in calling things by their correct names.* I watch Joey's hand move from bowl to bowl at the restaurant, as I float in a limbo of wondering why I'm stalling my answer to the Dean, why I'm not jumping at the chance, my only chance. My window of opportunity, the Dean had said, as if I was buying insurance. Joey, humming tonelessly, picks up what he needs, in a handful, a pinch, a ladleful, watching the contents in the wok and then jerking his wrist with calm precision, and suddenly he has made an omelette.

On Chinese New Year, the shop glittering with red and gold decorations, Eddie calls me into the kitchen and with much ceremony presents me with a moon cake.

'Good luck!' he says. 'Story of this is that wise woman sent message in the moon cake. The guards never think to look inside the cake. The woman was smarter than all of them. Inside, you eat it and see.' He and Joey and the other shy Chinese kitchenhand I know as Henry watch me as I raise the cake to my mouth and take a bite. It tastes like solid lard, a mashed slice of fat and sugar. My throat tightens.

I take a breath and chew, moving the texture around my mouth, thinking of jasmine tea and coriander, lemon juice to cut the grease, something hot and astringent to wash this down. I swallow.

'Mmmm …' I say. Their faces wreathe in smiles, nodding and grinning for me to continue.

I am twenty years old, and I will never teach in a university. I will withdraw from my honours proposal and drive alone to Cairns, where I will fall backwards off a boat holding goggles and a mask to my face, into eighteen metres of reef-fringed water and another element entirely. I will float weightless and astonished, my vision crammed with the lesson of what is always under the surface. *The fiercest dragon curls around its treasure. Burn the candle only when you need the light.* This is the first day of that journey north, the day I stand in the fragrant chaos of Eddie Lim's kitchen. I never find out what language they speak to each other as they work, but I ask their real names and they draw them for me in sharp characters on the back of a docket, flushing with pleasure.

'Delicious,' I say to a beaming ring of faces, and bite again. Fat coats the inside of my mouth, but it is so simple, this gesture of chewing and swallowing, savouring something so unfamiliar—a fin, a feather, a nest—all these remnants of flight and current.

'And look!' crows Eddie over the laughter of four displaced people. I glance inside the chunk of crumbling cake in my hand to see a hard-boiled egg yolk. I smile in recognition as I look at it, this dense, hidden message. How strange that this is the correct name for the thing, a moon cake, when my first glimpse through swimming vision convinces me I am staring at a tiny, buried, golden sun. How strange and gentle and quiet it is, learning to name something.

Wheelbarrow Thief

Stella lights the candles.

'Looks beautiful, darling,' says Daniel. He grabs and kisses the top of her perfumed head as she hurries past. 'Thanks so much for this. I mean it. You're amazing.'

But Stella is gone, choosing CDs and inserting them into the random play shuffle, putting more splintery pieces of red gum on the fire (kneeling carefully in her most flattering short black dress), and then casting another assessing eye over the table. She looks approvingly at the lyrical simplicity of the lacquer bowls and chopsticks, the only colour on the table the five gerberas, so vividly pink and orange that she feels slightly nauseated. Daniel must not know about the nausea. Must not guess until after this dinner, when she can pour them both a Cointreau and break the news to him, watching his eyes. Stella has been fighting nausea all day, and didn't it say in her book it would only last until the end of the morning?

Sipping lemon and water in the afternoon, she has taken each slimy piece of squid and washed it and felt along the rubbery seam for the clear spine of cartilage like a little transparent wing, and slivered each piece and brushed it with wasabi. Another sip of lemon water and then rolling up the nori rolls around that glutinous rice, raw shreds of salmon, the smallest line of shaved carrot. Stella has had to stop several times, her throat full of the sensory overload of raw fish, her tongue squirming in her mouth. But now, look. Perfection. Each piece a poem. Each messy gut and tail and vein discarded, wrapped in newspaper and safely in the bin.

Daniel will be flushed and expansive. *I have some news*, she will begin, her hair falling against her face by the firelight, *I know it is unexpected news, for you as well as for me …*

Stella swallows, wonders if she could be wearing too much perfume. 'Is this scent too strong?' she asks Daniel, who stops her, nuzzles into her neck, licks a line up to her earlobe.

'Hmm … no, I don't think so … just let me check this bit again …' They giggle together. Stella feels a pulsing drag deep inside her, a slow-motion somersault.

'Oh my God, I have to blanch the vegetables for the tempura.'

'Not in that stunning dress, surely. You're a vision, sweetheart.'

She smiles.

Champagne for when the guests arrive. The professor and his wife punctual to the moment, so Stella lets Daniel pour the drinks while she slips out to the bathroom to check whether she needs just a touch more blusher. Her eyes in the mirror are glittering. She brushes her hair up off her face and sprays it with volumiser. The scent hits her somewhere in the back of her mouth. She leans on the edge of the tiled sink, and gags. The doorbell. More of them are arriving.

'No, it's Stella's apartment,' Daniel is saying. 'Much grander than a struggling doctorate student could afford.'

'But Daniel spends a lot of time here,' Stella adds with a smile. She and Daniel have always referred to it as a flat. Large and old, it has two bedrooms, one of which was recently vacated by her ex-housemate Helen. Stella has meant for some weeks to advertise the room, so that the rent becomes more affordable, but this last week she has found herself standing in its doorway, watching the light fall into the empty space, trying to envisage it piled with Daniel's books, a desk, a lamp. Her mind treads down the path nervously, craning to see ahead. A cot.

'Also,' Daniel continues, refilling glasses, 'Stella's life is civilised enough to have not only a dining room, but six matching chairs. Isn't she lovely?'

Daniel goes on living at the university, he has told her, because he needs the privacy for his work and he wants tenure. He can attend functions, keep an ear to the ground, make himself a permanent presence on campus so that he will seem a natural choice for a position. He tells her this on a Sunday morning, lounging on her bed eating croissants and reading the paper, which she has slipped out early to buy, looking so much a fixture there, so familiar and in place, that it makes her want to weep with frustration.

He is listening with the appearance of deference now to the visiting Fellow, underdressed in that careless academic way in a shrunken fair-isle vest and colourless corduroys. Daniel listens and nods, squeezes his hands between his knees, looking at the floor with a small smile on his face. Everyone in the room except Stella mistakes this for respectful attention. The fact that she knows better, that she has seen him sprawled naked in the morning, dozing, and ragged-breathed with desire, quells her apprehension.

'And what do you do, Stella?' asks the professor's wife, whose name, in her nervousness, Stella has forgotten.

'I am a publicist.'

'Oh, that must be interesting.'

'Well ...' Stella takes a breath. At this moment, she knows, she is still mysterious. There is still the possibility of wit and assurance; she could now simply by opening her mouth and saying the right thing command the surprised attention of the whole room. Daniel's pretty girlfriend, and do you know she had the most interesting stories ...

'Yes,' she says, 'it is.' The professor's wife looks a kind woman. Stella is aware that she has published a volume of poetry and that she is involved in the university Dramatic Society. Stella has managed large productions that she knows this woman has dressed up to see in the city. She has some tales to tell of stars' tantrums, some choice morsels of backstage gossip and hair's-breadth financial cliffhangers, which would give her the floor right through the tempura and yakanori. She could divert the conversation like a river from the discourse of metaphysical poetry to something in which only she had insider knowledge. Stella considers this power, holds it concealed like a rabbit in a hat.

'It can get a bit hectic, though,' she says.

And feels poised attention shift back, sliding away on another current altogether.

I don't care, thinks Stella, putting her hand over her champagne glass as Daniel does the rounds again. *I can relinquish this easily, easily.* The thought of conception has shrunk the importance of the status of work. She even catches herself thinking of it as the job she used to have, an old role. Underpinned with conception, even the discourse of metaphysical poetry seems an etcetera. There is a hotter vein running under it now, a molten lode which heaves up, causing fault lines, cave-ins. Stella hugs the chaos to herself. This is not a discourse. It will never be reduced to discussion.

Stella seats herself last at the table, and lifts her spoon of clear soup. A gust of seaweed assails her nose, the smack of a wave under a pier, piles of kelp and mermaid's necklace crusty in the sun.

'Delightful,' pronounces the visiting Fellow, and she catches Daniel's loving eye. It has been worth it, making the stock from scratch. She had to read the recipe several times; surely she wasn't meant to throw out all the vegetables she had sliced according to directions? But she sees now, what seemed like waste is actually a kind of gift. Something reduced to its essentials, a sum total strained of its parts. Stella bathes in the appreciative silence, concentrates on keeping hers down.

In the kitchen a little while later, she hears Daniel's voice rise, the professor's respond, the professor's wife interject something flippant and conciliatory. When the visiting Fellow begins to rumble dogmatically, Stella's fingers tremble over the hot oil. There is going to be an argument.

The oil turns slickly in the wok. She drops in a tiny spoon of batter to test the heat, and watches it sizzle, prepares the plates with radish flowers and cucumber. She drops battered vegetables into the oil, fishes them out when they're golden onto absorbent paper. Her stomach pitches and tosses at the sight of so much grease. Perspiration stands on her forehead. *I am pregnant*, she thinks. *This is how it feels, this seasick, heavy ache.*

She hears the professor tap the table for emphasis, it sounds like someone knocking on a chest checking for false sides. She moves back into the dining room, bearing a platter of tempura. Each piece is golden and crisp, and she moves around the table selecting some for each plate, thanking the women as they praise her skill. The three men, staring at each other's mouths, waiting for their chance to speak with barely disguised impatience, hardly notice. Daniel pauses, looks down at his black lacquer chopsticks as if they, and the food he must eat with them, are something in a museum.

Stella bends her head to a secondary conversation started by the Fellow's wife, her eyes drawn again and again to the gerberas, so vivid they could be cartoon flowers.

'Ah, I have a story for you,' Daniel says, swallowing wine. Stella glances up and is in love with his face in the candlelight. The argument is dissipated—this is what academics do, there is no need to be upset. She knows the story he will tell; they have read it together in a volume of Zen parables that morning in a bookshop. Daniel, instead of finishing his mouthful, scoops another piece of sushi between his lips, and talks around it.

'There was once a man who worked in a factory, a very cunning man. The factory owners had heard rumours that he was a thief. And every day when he left the factory, he would be wheeling a wheelbarrow heaped full with sawdust.'

Stella experiences a shock of realisation that Daniel has recalled the story word for word. She herself, preoccupied with a lurching stomach, with packages of fish, with nerves, had barely skimmed it. Daniel takes another piece of raw salmon, scrapes off the wasabi, eats it. Inside her, Stella imagines another fish, eight weeks old and gilled, clamped, trembling. *I have some news, sweetheart, unexpected for me as well as for you …*

'Anyway, each day the guards sift through the sawdust, suspiciously looking for things he might have stolen. And each day there is nothing there but sawdust, and they wave him through the gates.'

You'll have your doctorate in November, we'll have a whole three months to get ready. Who knows how it happened? Who knows how anything happens. Don't you ever feel your body might take the decision out of your hands for a reason?

'Finally ...' Daniel pauses for effect, making eye contact with each of them. 'Finally they realise he is stealing wheelbarrows.'

They clap, they smile appreciatively. Laughter should not greet a Zen parable; it is not that kind of punchline. Daniel grins at Stella. He will be a great lecturer. He scissors another piece of sushi in his mouth, chewing as casually as if it were a French fry.

Stella had reached a point, with that raw salmon, where it had ceased to become food. Shaving it with the cleaver, she had seen it reduced to a single dense slab of flesh, of matter. Twenty-seven dollars, but it contained no secrets, nothing precious, nothing worth fetishising, despite the pompous mystique. Even the fishmonger at the market had lifted it away deferentially, handling it with almost a caress. It is ridiculous. It is quite right that Daniel—in fact, all of them—should eat each laboured-over morsel with such carelessness. She had had one piece, and the feverish image had risen in her mind that she was devouring a sliver of pressed tongue. Yes, perhaps she is feverish. The gerberas are positively oscillating in their own radiance, five flowers so perfect you could hardly believe in them.

'Coffee?' says Stella, rising in her beautiful black dress, steadying herself with the thought of a cold face cloth to the neck and forehead. Just through the kitchen, and into the bathroom. Then in a half-hour they will be gone, and she can break her news on the cusp of this dinner's success, on the gentle end of a wave, the battle over, the shore in sight.

'Would anybody care for chocolates?' she says, and as she moves past Daniel she feels him give the flesh of her backside a squeeze. Stella thinks of the magician's assistant, keeping things seamless. She thinks of the fishmonger.

She wipes her face, brushes her hair. Deep inside her, a ratchet is tightening up, each new calibration a metal nip of pain. 'I just want to spew,' she says to her reflection, and the word, so immediate and earthy, seems as shocking as *fuck*. How would it sound in the rarefied company of the dining room?

Her throat is tight as she re-enters that atmosphere, heavy by now with cigarette smoke and words, a sickening broth of indifference. Nobody asks her where she has been; nobody asks her opinion.

I might be a dummy, thinks Stella, wonderingly. *I might be made of sawdust.*

'Marvellous meal,' says the visiting Fellow to her lover who has spent the afternoon reading a book. Daniel, smiling genially, says, 'Oh, I didn't do much.'

'Yes, thank you so much,' says the professor's wife to Stella, and Stella can tell by the odd stumbled inflection that the woman has meant to say her name, but has forgotten it. *And why shouldn't she*, thinks Stella, holding the edge of the table. *I am just someone with a dining-room table and six chairs. I am something you sift in passing, looking for something worth having.*

'Goodnight,' she says. 'Goodbye.'

Stella kicks off her shoes and treads back unsteadily to the bathroom. Unwillingly, because it is dawning on her, with an exhausted certainty, what she will find there. She knows what the pain is now, feels it sharpen into something recognisable. That tilting drag, her queasiness, that accumulation of tension on the verge of becoming something else. Its familiarity springs her like a punchline, her obtuseness seems almost hilarious. Her teeth are chattering. As she unzips and steps out of her dress she observes her own devious body, its skipped cycle last month like a blank shrug. She sees her mistake. Her fingers skim her belly, one hand reaches between her legs, and then moves before her face fluttering with a bright flag of blood. She will not need to say her lines about the body making choices. This body, her body, has already hidden and then disclosed, revealed itself palm upwards. It is not a vehicle for carrying something else. Stella sits drained and naked on the toilet, and bleeds.

She hears, some minutes later, Daniel's solicitous knock.

'You okay, darling?' he says from the other side of the door.

Be careful, Stella tells herself. *He is cunning.* 'Yes, just a bit sick,' she answers.

'Could it have been the raw salmon?'

'No. Just ...'

'Women's troubles?'

Prudish bastard. Fool.

'Yeah. Would you mind going? I'm really tired.'

She can feel him weighing it up behind the door, frowning.

'Sure, if you think you'll be okay. Call you first thing?'

There is a pause. Stella feels her insides contract and unclench like a pulse, the fist turning into a hand.

'Goodnight,' she calls. 'Goodbye.'

Stella runs the bath. She will not be home first thing. She will be at the café, drinking pale China tea and writing an ad for the window, advertising the room. Thinking about it now, she savours it, a distilled flavour, runs her hands down her breasts and hips and legs. She is all here, and the cramp is lifting off her like steam.

Sea Burial

There's something so quiet and dignified about a burial at sea. It wasn't exactly that Alan had had a nautical past, but he'd loved the ocean. Loved that little yacht of his.

Up at Port Douglas he was never off the water, given half a chance. When I came in here just then and let myself into the silent house, it made me realise how very final death is. A cliché, I know, but true.

I'm glad I went with my instinct, and not decided on an ordinary plot. I don't know how people stand it — walking away leaving a loved one to be pressed under forever by damp clay. Instead I felt light. Divested, somehow. Oh, I was drained, certainly, but with what my new book from the library calls *closure*. Just a final goodbye, and a slip away. Beautiful.

I should have had time to get used to the quiet of the house, what with Alan away for weeks at a stretch in Singapore with his business. His business. Right up until the actual Commission Inquiry, I foolishly believed his business was the importation of woodcarvings. I swallowed everything he told me. Must have been a laughing stock. Even Alan realised at the end it was pointless even calling me as a witness.

So. The Philippines, doing God knows what, or else up in Queensland gambling with his cronies.

The ladies who came for bridge were always sympathetic about his absences. 'I don't know how you put up with it,' they'd say, when I told them Alan was away again, stocking up on new carvings.

The truth was, I'd gotten used to it. I had the house, of course, which meant I had the beach, and plenty of what Alan called play money. I had fresh freesias ordered every three days from the florist. So expensive, freesias, but they're my favourite flowers. I'd sit there looking at them, inhaling their perfume, and marvelling at the strangeness of fate.

When you think that only four years ago, after all, I'd had to borrow money for everything. Even for the funeral. Imagine that. My own daughter, and I had to have her cremated because it was cheaper. Borrowed money for the flowers, too — oriental lilies. Twenty-two dollars. They're too powerful, those flowers, aren't they? The scent. Stood there breathing in that sickly sweetness as I wept. Didn't shed a tear today for Alan; funny, isn't it? Completely dry-eyed. But then, I had closure.

Lilies are expensive flowers too, of course, but they're death flowers. Freesias are like a luxurious, perennial spring.

I loved arranging them, loved sitting on the leather divan with my nails done and a pile of glossy new magazines, carefully tearing open the sample perfume sachets. I'd subscribe to all the expensive ones. *Country Life. Vogue* and *Vanity Fair* and everything.

I was comfortable.

Comfortable — now there's a good word.

'I'm only thinking of your comfort.' That's what Alan would say in his wounded voice when I complained how often he was away, how I was marooned there in the beach-house.

'Sorry, sweetie,' Alan would say shortly, 'but business is business.'

And he bought me a cocker-spaniel puppy before he took off again. Within three months all the wives in the bridge club had one. There we'd sit, talking about puppy preschool and our husbands' heart medication, lining the mantelpiece with photos of our dogs.

'Never say you're rich, say you're comfortable,' instructed my mother, the instant expert, like someone who watches a game but never gets to play. She saw my marriage to Alan, my door into a new life, as her own leg-up into the upper echelons. My wedding day was the happiest day of her life. When she found out that Alan had hired the same florist as the one who did the Packer wedding, she cried tears of real joy.

So here I was, comfortable. Thanks to Alan, who was also supremely comfortable.

In fact, the only time I ever saw Alan uncomfortable

was when he was subpoenaed. There he was on the stand in his thousand-dollar suit and his face so florid and uneasy. He visibly winced at the word 'trafficking'. It offended his sensibilities. Well, Alan always kept his hands clean. He knew the value of good staff. Someone else opened doors, someone else changed gears. It's only good sense to have someone else who signs cheques. He was a businessman. The trouble was that woodcarvings were not, in the end, the business.

But he was confident that things would all be fixed up and he was right, of course. Alan had a broad range of acquaintances. He'd spent a good many years cultivating friends in high places, and quite a few in low. He'd survive.

No, what really bothered Alan after the inquiry, what really got him popping those heart tablets, was not the law, but someone outside the law, someone still on the outside with an axe to grind. I have to hand it to him. His instinct, as usual, was absolutely unerring.

I've been thinking today about the funeral, and me standing there holding the lilies, thinking my heart was going to break. I think maybe that it did break, or else something else broke. Something came away and drifted off like an empty boat.

It's the stupid little things, isn't it? What I couldn't stop crying at was the cheap yellow polyester lining of her coffin; all the tack and scrimping. Stapled onto the sides with a staple-gun. And her stick-thin arms. I hadn't seen her in a year, so it was a shock, still. And the powdery make-up they'd slapped on over the needle tracks. They could have matched her skin-tone, surely. Just shown a bit of love. That wouldn't have taken two minutes.

Poor Alan. In the end he just wanted a refuge, I suppose. I remember him arriving home last Wednesday after laying low in Port Douglas for two months. I know how he would have spent that time. Looking over his shoulder and doing a lot of business by phone. He was a nervous wreck. He looked a hundred. Waiting for the shoe to drop, I suppose.

Still, he played his part as best he could. Fumbling with the dog's leash, brightly suggesting an early-morning walk over the headland.

I took Goldie off the leash, though. Let her meander with me past the guardrail and down to the bluff. It wasn't the first time we'd done it. I suppose it does look dangerous, with the sheer drop and the waves crashing below. It's only natural he would follow.

Say what you like, it has dignity, a sea burial. So silent and elemental, and so few witnesses.

'Alan gone again?' That's what the bridge ladies will say tomorrow with that mock sympathy, and I'll nod with a mock regretful smile. Then I'll deal the cards.

Kill or Cure

'It's a lot of routine, I'm warning you,' John had said before they were married. 'You won't just be marrying me, you'll be marrying the place.'

'Can't wait,' she'd said. Helen remembered that night; exactly the way she'd said it as she'd leaned over the table. She'd had no idea, then, how much organising it had taken him just to have a weekend off in the city. She'd assumed once you planted stuff in the ground or put sheep out in a paddock, things basically took care of themselves.

'You won't know what to do with yourself,' her friends at work had said, not without a trace of envy, and she'd laughed.

'Watch me,' she'd smiled, raising her glass. She remembered that day, too; a great lunch in a good café where the owner knew her name. Funny the things you took for granted.

Now she watches John methodically chewing through a sandwich as she cuts up more cheese and tomato. As he eats he reads through the mail: the bank statements and veterinary bills she's collected for him that morning. The phone only rings now at mealtimes when people know he's going to be home: stock managers, reps, the CFA lieutenant, with some message about fertiliser or machinery or a meeting. At first, they'd rung all through the day, and she'd done her best to take everything down dutifully, pretending to know what they were talking about, but something's shifted there; word's got around.

Nothing else breaks the pattern of the day, not even weekends, when things go the same, only slower. When she visits the butcher, who's always friendly, she notices she has to be careful not to talk too much in what is often her biggest conversation with someone other than her husband for days. In town, she walks slowly down the quiet main street with its two pubs and three takeaways, the big new supermarket dumped at the end looking like a huge shiny toy. She glances into the hopeless little library with its old magazine collection and well-thumbed large-print westerns. She hasn't gone in there to sign a membership form. Not yet.

The old dog trains up the young dog, is what John explains.

'Up, Fella,' he says shortly to the old dog, whose adoration overcomes arthritis and bad hips, so that he determinedly hauls himself onto the tray of the ute. The new dog, in rangy puppyhood, watches nervously, then crouches and unfolds like a pocketknife to spring up alongside.

Helen watches them both there side by side amid the spades and ropes and coils of wire, as John starts up the ute and drives out of the yard. She watches the quaking balance of the young dog, which they've named Jake. It has to be a name you could shout, that the dogs can differentiate. Has to have a sharp consonant in it. Jake staggers on the ute tray, tail tucked between his legs, knobbly pelvis hunched into the air, looking miserably ahead as Fella drops his head over the side and relaxes.

Helen has to keep checking herself with the dogs. They aren't like pets. She stoops to give them a pat and they do a double take at her, then Fella breaks away uncomfortably to lie down nearby and Jake leans into her legs, overwhelmed by the unaccustomed attention. She feels John watching her, amused.

'The more you reward them for nothing,' he says, 'the less they'll obey you.' And it's true; they hesitate before coming when she calls, glancing uncertainly at John first. At nights they get fed and tied up, during the day they stick close to him, alert and anticipating every monosyllabic command. Jake has the genetic hard-wiring, just like Fella. The push, John calls it. It's something bred into them. They stay skinny and obsessive, focused only when John starts up the tractor or the chainsaw, or grabs the keys to go and move some sheep. A tremor seems to pass through their bodies then, like everything else is just waiting around. Fella rests with one ear up like an antenna. Jake can't settle, ever. He positions himself on the grass in front of the house, equidistant between the two doors, watching. Whichever one John comes out of, he's ready.

'Chooks okay?' says John, stirring his tea.

'Yeah, they're good.'

Three days before, she'd released the six new chickens into the run, the dogs observing her thoughtfully from the back of the ute. She'd ordered the birds from the produce store and spent a day shifting the old machinery cluttering up the shed and reinforcing the netting with new star pickets. The chickens had stepped through the overgrown run suspiciously, pecking here and there at shoots of green. At the show Helen's seen a rooster she wants—a big white cockerel with a brilliant red comb. And she'll make a temporary yard for them so they can scratch over the weed-choked vegetable patch, and then she'll put in some asparagus. The weeds have got away from her, she's the first to admit. Turn your back and they're up to your waist. She doesn't know where the days go. She'll put some asparagus in, and change those awful curtains in the guest room, and then she'll invite some friends up from the city.

She stacks plates in the sink now, and catches sight of the two dogs out the kitchen window. Jake's still sitting at his post, gazing through the glass with rapt gleaming attention at John eating, waiting to jump on command.

'That dog's got to learn to relax,' she says jokingly as John stands to go, and he grins and lifts her hair, kisses her on the back of her neck.

'He's a kelpie,' he says. 'They never relax. They're like the class prefect.'

He's out the door with one more sandwich, and as she starts washing plates, she can hear the dogs' claws hit the metal as they scrabble back into the ute. She finds herself idly reading the label on the washing-up liquid, and shakes her head impatiently. No wonder, like a couple of acolytes, the dogs idolise John, with his wordless, unequivocal sense of purpose and order, his day full of small objectives, the onward roll of tyres.

Every couple of nights she kneels next to him on the verandah, holding the dogs steady as he methodically checks for grass seeds in their paws and coats. The dogs submit to his ministrations stiffly, tucking their tails up between their legs and looking away as he carefully separates their toes. She feels their ribs move under his fingers as he finds corkscrew grass in tufts of hair and inside their ears. Covertly, she watches his slow, hard hands working through their fur. When they'd talked about getting married she'd taken him to meet her parents, and as she was gabbling nervously at the table she'd felt his hand move to the small of her back and stay there, the silent, soothing pressure of his palm warm through her silk shirt.

'Well,' her father had said to her later, 'there's a bloke who's not going to waste his time on small talk.' And Helen had imagined the two of them working together, heads close and no need for words; some enviable, shared comprehension.

'Hey, Jakey,' she whispers now, cuddling the young dog to her, smelling his clean, grassy smell. Jake's going to love her, she's decided. She scratches him behind the ears, and he collapses, sagging and boneless, across her knees.

Constantly, it seems, she needs to get a broom and brush down the cobwebs that keep appearing in the house. She'll be lying in bed and notice fine webs around the windows shining in the sun, in places she's only swept clean days before. Narrow spiders repair them incessantly, their crooked legs in constant circular motion. Around the lights they construct elaborate web traps, throwing disconcerting, hugely magnified shadows on the walls. She rotates the broom slowly, collecting the spider webs like sticky spun sugar from every crevice and insect path.

Helen can't believe, now, how housework can consume her day, how the weeds outside can get so out of hand so quickly, how she's up a ladder washing windows instead of at the desk in the study, writing query letters for some freelance work. All she's done at that desk, so far, is steer her way through the clunky computer program they use to do the farm books, sitting in the big antique chair that had belonged to John's father. The computer hum and the clock are the only sounds in the room. On the smallest pretext, she drives herself into town.

'Going to be a big year for fires, you reckon?' says the butcher, wrapping up her meat in white paper as she lingers in the shop.

'Well, after that wet spring, probably,' she answers. Something she's heard John say, as he stands looking at the paddocks drying off.

'Yep. Total fire ban, soon.' He slides the cabinet shut.

'We won't be needing to get these free-range eggs from you much longer. Did I tell you I got some chickens last week?' she says suddenly, and his genial face slides from the next customer waiting and back to her, courteously patient.

'Is that right?'

The other customer looks at her, curious, and she smiles quickly and says goodbye. *Jesus, I'm pathetic*, she tells herself, slinging the shopping into the car and sliding in. Next to where she's parked, one of the takeaway cafés has a sign advertising *cuppachinos*. She'd smirked at this when she'd first come to town, but six months of meeting no one to have one with has wiped the grin off her face. The joke had been on her after all, thinking she could afford to be condescending.

The next morning, John and the dogs are long gone by the time she takes the compost scraps down to the chicken yard. It's silent. Inside, she finds all six of them strewn across the enclosure, dead. Their bodies seem deflated somehow; limp as rags, feathers scattered through the weeds. Trembling, she finds the spot where a dog has scraped away one of the bricks she's wedged in, and dug a hole wide enough to wriggle under.

When John comes back midmorning she tells him what's happened and finds she has to keep her voice from shaking.

'They're just all torn up,' she says finally, 'just thrown around.' She turns to look accusingly at Jake, who gazes back at her with total, oblivious incomprehension. His tongue lolls with goodwill.

'There's an old antidote for it,' John says after lunch as he gets the shovel to bury the chickens. 'It's like a kill or cure thing. Like aversion therapy.' He takes one of the dead birds and ties it to Jake's collar. The dog's cautious interest in proceedings turns to nervous incredulity, his paws skidding desperately as John yanks him into the chicken shed and ties him up on a short rope. There, he strains and chokes, his eyes rolling in panic, fighting the rope. The chicken's neck lolls and flops like a broken toy.

'Now we leave him,' John says.

'You're joking.'

'Theory is that the dog associates the smell of the dead chook with being exiled, or something—he never wants to go near them again.'

Jake's frenzied barking doesn't begin until he hears the ute start up when John leaves for the yards again. Then Helen thinks he might strangle himself, or have a fit. She can hear him in there, like someone having a nightmare, pulling and gagging at the rope, howling for release, hour after hour. Finally, just to get away from it, she gets in the car and goes into town to collect the mail and do some shopping, and hides in the air-conditioned library for as long as she can, thumbing through gardening magazines. As soon as she arrives home, though, the dog hears her car door and starts up again.

When she hears the ute pull finally into the drive she runs out and grabs John's arm.

'I can't stand it,' she says. 'Let him off, for godsakes. I'll fix the fencing. Just let him off.'

He looks at her for a long moment. 'You're making a rod for your own back,' he says, taking off his hat and throwing it into the tray. 'It's the way the cure works. Don't think of it as cruel, Helen. It's only for a day or two. I heard of an old farmer once, grabbed one of the feathers and wired it onto the dog's jaw so it stayed tickling the back of its throat for hours. Never went anywhere near a chook again.'

She stares at him, feeling hot saliva flood her mouth, her own throat closing and gagging like a reflex.

'Let him off,' she says tightly, and turns away.

She hears Jake's barking change to whining hysteria as John goes over, his mouth set in its taciturn line of disapproval, and unties the rope. The dog bows before him, obsequious as a penitent before a god.

A week later, galvanised with fresh energy, she cleans the house of new webs and decides to tackle the fencing again. She will set the reinforced wire into a trough of cement, then bend extra chicken wire out from the base to make it impossible for the dogs, or a fox, to dig in. It will be impenetrable, safe from predation, and then she will buy more chickens and the rooster, and start afresh.

She takes the shovel from where it's leaning against the shed, and begins digging what she envisages will be a long trench around the enclosure. But even after what seems like hours, when she comes back after going inside for a drink of water, sweaty and light-headed, she can't believe how shallow the hole is that she's managed to scrape out. She sucks her blisters and sits back on the porch, her enthusiasm baked dry and shrivelled in the heat. John sees what she's been doing when he comes home for lunch; notes the puny pile of dry dirt and the abandoned tools.

'You'd be better off using the square-edge spade for that,' is his only comment. 'It's sharper.' His hand reaches for the stack of mail as he sits down.

Helen nods, and takes out more slices of bread. After this, she'll do another load of washing then cut up the steak in the fridge for tonight. Used to be the butcher would do that for her, free of charge, as they chatted. But last time she'd gone in there they'd hardly spoken. He must have seen her in the previous week, carrying the two polystyrene trays of discounted chops she'd bought on impulse at the supermarket, because he'd stared out at the street behind her, pointedly offhand, as she talked to him. 'Anything else?' he'd said finally, wrapping up the steak quickly and clapping the parcel with finality onto the counter. She'd broken off, confused, and handed him the money as she shook her head.

'Regards to John,' he'd said shortly as she went out.

She's just cooking the rice when the phone rings. John answers and runs a hand tiredly over his jaw.

'Sorry, Hel. Just put mine in the oven. There's some sheep out on the road up McKenna's lane; they must have slipped under at the creek. I'll have to go before it gets too dark.'

He doesn't ask her to come and help, she notices.

Assumes she'll sit here useless, reading her library book. She follows him outside, where the sun is setting in a drenching sea of red over the paddocks. Crickets fly up around their legs in the dusk, and tinder-dry grass crunches to powder beneath their shoes.

'I'll take Fella in the cabin for once,' he says, opening the passenger door, 'less distance to jump for him.' Fella scrambles up stiffly, goes straight to the floor and curls there as if not pushing his luck. So perfectly devoted, thinks Helen, watching him tuck his tail in quickly so it doesn't get caught in the door, so grateful for every small concession. She's pulling the gate open when she senses Jake floundering through the fence and coming up behind her.

For a fleeting second she has an idea the dog is waiting for her command. She imagines him pushing his head briefly into her hand, a small communiqué of devotion, like he does with John. The padding feet approach behind her, and then suddenly she feels teeth nip her heel sharply and Jake slinks away again into the shadows. It takes her a long, astounded moment to realise the dog has actually bitten her.

'Come here!' she calls angrily, hearing her voice crack as she raises it. The dog skirts her in a wide semicircle, sharply outlined in the dusk, then gives her one sly contemptuous sidelong glance before leaping carelessly into the back of the ute.

John, not noticing, gives her a small wave as he drives out. When Helen snaps on the light in the bathroom a few minutes later to find some disinfectant, she sees her jeans and socks are studded with dozens of grass seeds, twisted like perfectly formed screws into the fabric, designed to go in and never come out.

When he finally returns she is sitting on the floor in the laundry, grimly going through their socks and picking out the embedded corkscrew grass. Summer hasn't even really hit yet; she'll have months of this ahead. *Get used to it,* she tells herself. *You wanted it, now put up or shut up.* The tightness in her shoulders, the ache from her pointless bout of digging, pulls her neck down, and she leans back against the cool brick of the laundry wall, her throat filling. She hears John pull his boots off one by one and slide open the screen door, and can tell from his footfalls up the hall to bed how tired he is.

She can hear it in his voice, too, when she climbs into bed herself, red-eyed and sniffing, an hour later.

'What's wrong?' he says. No alarm there, just the tone of someone whose energy is spent, facing more unwelcome work. Someone with no interest in small talk. She can hear what it costs him to even broach that silence.

'Nothing,' she says. 'Nothing.' She sees the blue eyelid pulled over the staring dead eye of a chicken, a roll of rippling yellow fat where the dog has held the body down with one paw and ripped upwards with those teeth. The dog's fervour turned to revulsion, pawing at the carcass tied to him. She hears the cargo train bang through the station at 3.20 a.m., the sound rolling up the creek bed, metal striking metal.

She's sure she can hear the dog barking too, echoing and distant, a rhythmic, maddening bark. She strains her ears.

Bloody Jake. Must have slipped his chain.

She slides out of bed and walks to the back door, feeling new webs break across her face and arms; freshly repaired webs, looping like a trapeze from wall to wall, untiring and remorseless.

But the dog is there; a dark shape curled nose to tail, sound asleep at the other end of the porch. Helen sits on the arm of the couch and raises her foot in her hand. Hardly broken the skin, really. Just that single puncture on the heel where one curved tooth's penetrated, red and raised. Itching now.

It's only after she has returned to bed and listened again to that distant metronomic barking that it occurs to her that it's no dog she can hear, but her husband's breathing, faint next to her and sunk into his pillow, catching with a small sound each time he exhales.

It follows her into sleep, that flat insistent rhythm. It's like someone resolutely and patiently striking the same match, over and over, ready to stoop and set a stubble field alight.

Acknowledgements

For the sheer pleasure of their talent, thanks to Peter Temple, Tim Winton, Paddy O'Reilly, Kate Grenville, Carrie Tiffany, Peter Carey and so many others.

For their enthusiastic response to my early attempts, thanks to the Sisters in Crime.

For the cup of tea placed thoughtfully at my elbow, thanks to Dave Dore.

The Stories

What Thou and I Did, Till We Loved won *The Age* Short Story Competition, 2001 (published in *The Age*)

A Pitch Too High for the Human Ear won third prize in the University of Canberra Short Story Competition, 1997 (published in *Behind the Front Fence*, Five Mile Press, 2004)

Habit won *The Age* Short Story Competition, 2000 (published in *The Age*, and in *On The Edge*, Five Mile Press, 2005)

Flotsam won the University of Canberra Short Story Competition, 2002 (published in *Island*, and in *Secret Lives*, Five Mile Press, 2003)

Cold Snap won the *HQ*/Sceptre Short Story Prize, 2001 (published in *HQ*)

Resize was shortlisted in the *HQ*/HarperCollins Short Story Competition, 1996 (published in *Enter*, HarperCollins, 1997)

The Testosterone Club was a prizewinner in the Scarlet Stiletto Awards, 1995

Angel was highly commended in the University of Canberra Short Story Competition, 1997

The Light of Coincidence won the *Herald Sun*/Rotary Short Story Competition, 1996 (published in the *Herald Sun*)

Soundtrack won second prize in the University of Canberra Short Story Competition, 2002

Direct Action won second prize in the Glen Eira Short Story Award, 2002 (published in *Meanjin*)

The Correct Names of Things won the University of Canberra Short Story Competition, 1997 (published in *Redoubt*)

Wheelbarrow Thief was shortlisted in the *HQ*/HarperCollins Short Story Competition, 1996 (published in *Enter*, HarperCollins, 1997)

Sea Burial was broadcast on ABC Radio National (in a slightly different form) and included on their double CD of *Australian Stories*

Dark Roots, *Seizure* and *Kill or Cure* are all new, previously unpublished stories

Dark Roots

Cate Kennedy

ABOUT THIS GUIDE

We hope that these discussion questions
will enhance your reading group's exploration
of Cate Kennedy's *Dark Roots*. They are
meant to stimulate discussion, offer new viewpoints,
and enrich your enjoyment of the book.

More reading group guides and additional information,
including summaries, author tours, and author sites for
other fine Grove Press titles, may be found on
our Web site, www.groveatlantic.com.

QUESTIONS FOR DISCUSSION

1. "I have been told, both in approval and in accusation, that I seem to love all my characters. What I do in writing of any character is to try to enter into the mind, heart, and skin of a human being who is not myself. Whether this happens to be a man or a woman, old or young, with skin black or white, the primary challenge lies in making the jump itself. It is the act of a writer's imagination that I set most high."
—Eudora Welty

   Do you think Kennedy seems to love all her characters? Does she enter completely into "the mind, heart, and skin" of different people? Do you, as a reader, feel drawn to follow her there? Which characters in these stories do you understand and feel the best, whether or not you condone their actions?

2. Did you find that the stories offer a surprising range of subjects, tones, and settings? Most are focused on one relationship or a family. Yet think about the variety of human natures and conflicts. The spirit may be sly satire or grim vengeance or just endurance, but usually with ironic insights. Which stories use shock value effectively? Which ones make you smile with satisfaction, perhaps along with the narrator?

3. Violence, real or imagined, is often a place of revelation or a sharp turning point. Think of the accident in "What Thou and I Did, Till We Loved." And the near murder in "Flotsam." Recall the sustained imagery of trapping that leads to the final event in "Cold Snap." What other stories turn on a violent act?

4. Crimes can be blatant or subtle in the stories. Do you think some are even debatable? Eco-crime in "Direct Action" is a destructive yet justifiable act of civil disobedience in the eyes of the perpetrator. And in those of the reader? What about the border smuggling in "Habit"? Where on the scale would you put the pickling episode in "The Testosterone Club"? And how about letting the dog loose in "Sea Burial"?

5. Is lack of communication, or, more dramatically, a failure to communicate something crucial at a crucial time, often the problem in flawed relationships in the stories? In each of them do you notice small, seemingly insignificant moments that might magnify a whole malaise in a relationship? "Oh Andrew, he never talks" (p. 16) in "A Pitch Too High for the Human Ear." In this story where does Andrew find his best communication? Does Kennedy allow us to feel sympathy for both husband and wife? Do you feel more empathy for a character with remorseful insight into his or her limitations? What does the title mean? And the forlorn last words, "*Can you hear it Vicki?* I want to say. It's not words, it's nothing so coherent as words. It's all of us, hoarse with calling, straining in the darkness to hear something we recognise as our names" (p. 22).

6. When do women make conscious choices to leave men in the stories? When do women decide to live their own lives instead of plumping up and being subsumed by men? How is Daniel portrayed in "Wheelbarrow Thief"? How does Stella's cuisine, especially her stock cooking, prefigure later events? ("But she sees now, what seemed like waste is actually a kind of gift. Something reduced to its essentials, a sum

total strained of its parts" p. 159). What gives Stella the strength to free herself? "Thinking about it now she savours it, a distilled flavour, runs her hands down her breasts and hips and legs. She is all here, and the cramp is lifting off her like steam" (p. 164). Talk about a similar liberation in "Seizure." Are certain traits shared by Steve and Daniel?

7. How does Monica start to preserve herself (preserve: an operative word in the story) by designating her husband and his two pals "The Testosterone Club"? What in their behavior merits this name? We read of "their complete confidence in their own majestic sexual magnetism" (p. 66). What is the tone of Monica's recollections? Is she appalled, amused, or threatened by the trio? How do Monica's talents as a can-do woman in the kitchen provide her highly satisfactory escape? How does her husband sow the mustard seed of his own destruction with his special gift to his wife? Does the story remind you a little of Alec Guiness's film *Kind Hearts and Coronets*?

8. Would you say that Cate Kennedy is shrewd about contrasting turbulent interior lives with threats from the outside world? Which stories explore this contrast most dramatically? Can the outside threats be imagined, as perhaps in "Dark Roots"? Is the narrator her own nemesis as she "spirals down" into deception? She calls it a "slippery slope" and "a poison," her fear of aging. "You have traded in your unselfconsciousness for this double-visioned state of standing outside yourself, watchful and tensed for exposure" (p. 84). Is there hope at the end for this May-October romance? What do you think will happen if she turns the light on?

9. In "Habit" when do we learn the sex of the narrator? Does withholding this information contribute to ambiguity in the story? Do we nonetheless learn quite a lot about the narrator through her internal monologue? How real is the menace at customs? How does it compare to the larger menace in the narrator's life? Talk about how sentences like "I seem to be inviting confession," "I have, I suppose, a habit," "it's the faith that heals," and "I am blessed" stitch together the story?

10. In "Cold Snap," how would you describe the boy's mental state? Is he somehow gifted with odd intuition even though he is limited in other ways? How are his love and understanding of trees important to the story? Is it appropriate that the feed-store boy refers to *Deliverance*? How does the father's revenge foreshadow the pattern of the story later, and does it create a sense of dread? How do the new people bring trouble on themselves? Comment on "Well, it looks like the light's on but there's no one home" (p. 52), "Look at all those bloody trees . . . I'm sick of the sight of them" (p. 53), and "I started explaining but she wasn't really listening" (p. 53). Do the woman's alien, exploitive values lead her to a trap? How does Billy use nature to ensnare "the loony lady" who is herself a threat to nature? "That's what nature's like, for everything poisonous there's something nearby to cure it if you just look around" (p. 57).

11. In "Resize", Dave as a husband feels bleak and inept. How does the imagery of removing the wedding rings ("He feels the moment heat up, become molten") alleviate his feeling baffled and numb? Is the shift buttressed by the clunker

of a car suddenly behaving? "He steps on the clutch and finds first gear, feeling the calibrations gnash like teeth momentarily then drop into place, lubricated, fitted together like bones in a hand" (p. 64). Talk about this shift of gears in the marriage.

12. Three of the stories set in motion the relationships of mothers and daughters. Explore the challenges, conflicts, and resolutions faced by both mothers and daughters in "Flotsam," "Angel," and "Soundtrack." The characters and settings are strikingly different. Do you see any points of comparison? Are there some elements of universality?

13. Flannery O'Connor has said that "a story always involves, in a dramatic way, the mystery of personality." Is that a useful way to look at the stories in *Dark Roots*? O'Connor further says that good stories are not triggered by problems or abstract issues but by concrete details and the five senses. Which of the stories leap to mind for the mystery of personality, concrete detail, and the senses? Can you give examples?

14. Motivation for characters' actions can be murky and deceptive. Often even the characters fail to understand why they do what they do . . . or fail to do. Auden has said, "The desires of the heart are as crooked as corkscrews." Do you understand what drives people in this book? Which ones still perplex you?

SUGGESTIONS FOR FURTHER READING:

A Few Short Notes on Tropical Butterflies by John Murray; *Where You Find It* by Janice Galloway; *Goodnight, Nobody* by Michael Knight; *Sightseeing* by Rattawut Lapcharoensap; the short fiction of Lorrie Moore, *The Dead Fish Museum* by Charles D'Ambrosio; *Everyman's Rules for Scientific Living* by Carrie Tiffany.